THE REIGN OF THE EVIL ONE

THE REIGN OF THE EVIL ONE

(Le Règne de l'Esprit Malin)

By CHARLES FERDINAND RAMUZ

Translated by JAMES WHITALL

Introduction by ERNEST BOYD

ONESUCH PRESS

LONDON   MELBOURNE   NASHVILLE

Onesuch Press enriches lives by reclaiming the forgotten past; publishing the lesser known works of great writers and the great works of forgotten ones. For more information about us visit www.onesuchpress.com.

A ONESUCH BOOK
Published by ONESUCH PRESS
PO Box 303BK, Black Hill 3350 Australia

National Library of Australia Cataloguing-in-Publication entry
Author: Ramuz, C.F. (Charles Fedinand), 1878 - 1947.
Title: The Reign of the Evil One/Charles Ferdinand Ramuz; translated by James Whitall; introduction by Ernest Boyd

ISBN: 978 0 9872760-5-6 *(pbk)*
ISBN: 978 0 9872760-6-3 *(ebook)*

Other Authors/Contributors
Whitall, James, 1888-
Boyd, Ernest

Dewey Number: 843.912

The paper used in this publication meets the minimum requirements of ANSI/NISO Z39.48-1992 (R1997) (Permanence of Paper). The paper used in this book is from responsibly managed forests. Printed in the United States of America, the United Kingdom and Australia by Lightning Source, Inc.

INTRODUCTION

It is probably safe to say that most English-speaking people are more familiar with the winter-sports of Switzerland than with its literature. Even those who are vaguely conscious of the Swiss birth of Rousseau, Vinet, Benjamin Constant, and Amiel, have never thought of them as part of a national Swiss literature. Nor have the writers of modern French Switzerland emerged any more clearly from the mainstream of French literature. A few readers may remember the nationality of Edouard Rod, which prevented his election to the French Academy. But how many living Swiss writers are known? When one has explored for many years a bypath of letters and made some interesting discoveries, it is at once gratifying and embarrassing to be called upon to justify one's weakness for adventuring outside the main-travelled roads of European literature. That is the position in which I find myself as I try to enlist interest in the work of C. F. Ramuz, whose name, I think, had never been publicly mentioned in English until I seized the excuse of his increasing fame in France within recent years to draw attention to this remarkable Swiss novelist. Like Anglo-Irish literature, the literature of Switzerland has inevitably been overshadowed by that of the more powerful neighbour whose language it used. It was when I sought out that literature, whose counterpart in Ireland I knew, not the expatriate but the autochthonous writers, that I entered upon a pleasant voyage of discovery.

Charles Ferdinand Ramuz, who was born at Lausanne in 1878, is one of the group of young French Swiss intellectuals who founded the *Voile latine* movement at Geneva in the autumn of 1904. At that time Edouard Rod was the only Swiss author; of more than local fame, and his reputation, like that of Cherbuliez before him, was essentially French, although in his later years he returned to Switzerland and associated himself more closely with the intellectual life of his own country. Ramuz and his friends, while agreeing with Rod's frank criticism of Swiss literature for its dullness, its provinciality, and its incurable moralising, could not accept him as their leader, for he was precisely the type of Parisianised Swiss against which the *Voile latine* group protested. Their avowed task was very similar to that of W. B. Yeats and his associates in Ireland thirty years ago. They wanted the art of Switzerland to be national, and they wished to set up aesthetic standards in place of the facile judgments of a public which accepted local celebrities for moral and patriotic reasons, but always looked to Paris for serious work.

The first number of the *Voile latine* appeared in October 1904, shortly after Ramuz had published his first book, a sheaf of poems collected under the title of *Le Petit Village*. Amongst the other contributors who have since become well-known were Gonzague de Reynold, the critic of the movement and recent biographer of Baudelaire, and Henry Spiess, a distinguished and delicate poet, whose work, with that of Ramuz, is the chief accomplishment of this renaissance of French-Swiss literature. Very soon the review attracted all the best talents, Louis Dumur, Madame Burnat-Provins, and Robert de Traz, who now edits *La Revue de Genève*. It ran until the end of 1910, and in 1914 its place was taken by *Les Cahiers vaudois*, designed after the plan of Charles Peguy's *Cahiers de la quinzaine*. This publication is now valuable and important, for in it Ramuz published all his work during several years: *Raison d'être*, essays half critical, half biographical; *Chansons*, a collection of poems; three

11

major works of fiction, *La Guerre dans le Haut Pays; Le Règne de l'Esprit Malin; La Guérison des Maladies*; and *Le Grand Printemps*, reflections upon the war. Most of these works have not been issued in any other form. The purpose of the *Voile latine* was to satisfy "the need of a renaissance which a few young writers of French Switzerland have felt, and to give complete freedom of self-expression to every individual." During the seven years of its existence La *Voile latine* represented a definite movement in the direction of national tradition in art and literature, a tradition at once Helvetian and Latin, classical and modern, above all, Swiss. It turned the creative and critical impulse towards the sources of nationality, and aimed at an art which, in all its branches, would be as truly of the soil as the mountains and chalets of Switzerland.

Although C. F. Ramuz began with the traditional little book of poems, to which he has since added *La Grande Guerre du Sondrebund* and *Chansons*, his fame rests entirely upon his work in prose fiction. His first novel, *Aline*, was published in 1905, and was followed by *Les Circonstances de la Vie* (1907), *Jean-Luc pérsécute* (1909), *Aimé Pache, peintre vaudois* (1911), and *La Vie de Samuel Belet* (1913). These represent a definite period in his development which seems to have terminated with the war, for since then his work has entered upon a new phase, of which *Le Règne de l'Esprit Malin* (The Reign of the Evil One) is the most brilliant illustration. His first period was one of realism, in which it appeared as if a successor to Rod had been found whose genius was wholly Swiss. In an early number of the *Voile latine*, when the eternal question was being debated as to whether there could really be a distinctively Swiss literature, Ramuz formulated the point of view from which his own position must be estimated. He reduced the role of French culture to one of pure aesthetics, looking to France, not for ideas but for models in the art of writing French. His novels and stories are as indigenous as the strongest nationalist could wish. He is not just another French author who happened to be born in Lausanne instead of Paris. He is more intensely and exclusively Swiss than Rod; at the same time he is not a mere parochial celebrity of the chocolate and Swiss milk variety, several of whom, it so happens, have long ago been translated into English! M. Ramuz is a writer in the same category as J. M. Synge and James Joyce, an artist whose appeal is universal, though the form and content of his work bear the deepest imprint of purely local and immediate circumstance.

There is, indeed, a suggestion of Synge in the method of M. Ramuz, at least in the earlier novels of his realistic period from *Aline* to *La Vie de Samuel Belet*. They spring from the very soil of the country in which the scene is laid, and are the creations of a mind which has adapted itself with great skill to the simplicity of the folk manner. As he sits in the village inn of some Swiss hamlet, his ear notes the turns of phrase, the savoury idioms of the country people. The slow rhythms of this speech possess him, and in this close contact with man and nature he gradually learns some half-forgotten legend, the fragment of an idyll or the vague tradition of a rustic tragedy. Then he has the theme of a novel, which he will proceed to elaborate in the deliberate, naive style of the narrators, reconstructing the fable piece by piece, with a scrupulous notation of every detail of time and place. The limitations of this method are obvious. There is a lack of spaciousness, of perspective, in these pictures filled with 'scarcely articulate figures, and where every detail is recorded with the same minute care. The art of M. Ramuz is essentially narrative and plastic, and his canvasses have the charm of the Primitives. *Aline* is a little peasant romance with a tragic denouement; *Jean-Luc persécuté* tells the story of drama of infidelity in a mountain village. In themselves they are trifles, but the author has recaptured the movement of life in them.

While those two books, together with *Nouvelles et Morceaux*, are peasant studies, pure and simple, revealing in their brevity the author's method, it is in his three long novels, *Les Circonstances de la Vie* (1906), *Aimé Pache, peintre vaudois* (1911), and *La Vie de Samuel Belet*, that M. Ramuz first showed his greatest power. Here the technique is the same, but it is applied to the richer material of provincial manners, in a country where the small town is nearer to the village than to the city, and where the absence of large cities makes it possible to contain the whole panorama of a people's life in this framework. *Les Circonstances de la Vie* may be called the history of a Swiss Charles Bovary, the ignominious defeat of a mediocre individual by the force of circumstances as ignoble as they are implacable. Emile Magnenat, the good, respectable, commonplace notary, is the central figure. With meticulous care M. Ramuz sets this character upon the stage, describes his social background, his wedding, his family, the family clergyman, and the rest. The German-Swiss servant Frieda Henneberg is the instrument of the katharsis which destroys all the secondhand morality and smug security of the family, when she establishes her domination over the man and finally ruins him. In *Aimé Pache* the same social stratum is examined, but the young artist is a more powerful character than poor Emile, his pursuit of his destiny is conscious and deliberate and he succeeds in mastering his own fate. The struggle of the artist, first against the bourgeois suspicions of his own people, his career as a student in Paris, and his painful groping towards the discovery that only by conforming to the deeper, racial impulse, by returning to the soil of his fathers, can he fully realise himself—such is the story.

What is of great interest in the work of C. F. Ramuz is its

analysis of the French Protestant mind, and the expression in literature of an element whose absence from the literature of France must always seem a loss to English readers. M. Andre Gide, it is true, betrays his Huguenot origins in his writings, but only the Swiss have produced a literature in which Protestantism is an influence as all pervading as in English. M. Ramuz has admirably preserved the Protestant note which, coupled with the familiar idiom of the country people in which he writes, lends a piquant contrast to his novels as compared with the very different atmosphere of French fiction. If the desires of the flesh are by no means a negligible part of his drama of Swiss life, how subdued and uneasy these sinners are! They have none of the abandon, or the frank animality, or the self-conscious ecstasy, of the people described by Maupassant, Flaubert, and the Goncourts. Aline, and *Aimé* Pache, and Emile Magnenat have the inhibitions of the Calvinistic tradition in their souls. They take their pleasure as sadly as the traditional Englishman. The puritan suspicion of joy pervades the communities of town and country of which M. Ramuz has made himself the interpreter. The rhythm of folk-speech alternates with that of the Bible, In *Les Circonstances* we read:

"*On va longtemps dans une vallée, et marcher est peut-être dur; toutefois il y a des pentes couvertes d'arbres, de la mousse, des sources fraîches, on peut se dire: 'ce sera plus beau de l'autre côté.' De sorte qu'il reste quand même un peu de joie au fond du coeur, laquelle excite à avancer. Mais on sort, on trouve une plaine de sel, et on sait qu'aussi loin qu'on pourra aller, ce sera toujours cette plaine, cette même stérilité; qu'est-ce qui nous reste? Plus rien.*"

The same Biblical note is heard in *Aimi Pache*, in a love scene which is quite the farthest removed from all that we are accustomed to expect in French fiction:

"*D'autres sont entrés dans la mort; moi j'en sors, et je me lève avec elle à la vie. Comme au temps d'Eve, avant la faute,—car, toute idée de faute était écartée d'eux, et toute possibilité de faute était écartée d'eux. Ce fut comme au temps d'Eve couchée sous le palmier, et Adam est couché près d'elle, et ils n'avaient point la notion du mal. Les biches venaient boire, elles étaient sans crainte. Il disait: 'Es-tu là?' Elle repondait, 'Je suis là.' Et il reprenait: 'Es-tu là?, et je sais bien que tu es là, mais répète-le-moi quand même, pour que ta voix soit aussi avec moi.' Et elle disait: 'Je suis là.'"*

The style of M. Ramuz is coloured by this inevitable Protestant influence which is so unlike the movement of the French prose of France. Add to that his deliberate cultivation of popular Swiss speech, which has a harshness and a lack of grace at times intolerable to the ear accustomed to the finely polished instrument of cultured French. His critics have not hesitated to warn M. Ramuz of the risk he incurs of forgetting the definite limitations of his method, and passages of great slovenliness have been cited against him. In this respect his last four volumes show him to be impenitent, but they have marked a new phase in his development. *Le Règne de l'Esprit Malin, Les Signes parmi nous,* and *La Guérison des Maladies,* were all three published by the group of *Les Cahiers vaudois,* and to them may be added his last novel, *Terre du Ciel* (1921), which is in the same manner. These stories are of a mystical rather than a realistic character, and suggest at times the apparently ubiquitous influence of Claudel. But M. Ramuz is faithful to his Swiss peasants, and what he gives us, for instance in *La Guérison* is a sort of Protestant Claudelism. One prefers the human tragedy of *Aline* to the mystico-religious study of the miracle-working Marie, who takes to herself the diseases of the village, until the unsympathetic authorities remove her to hospital. In *Les Signes* the author essays to give the air of mysterious portents to the threat of two sinister events, which throw their shadow over a prosperous community in war time. The one, which is never named, is an epidemic of "Spanish influenza," the other is "bolshevism." M. Ramuz gives a vigorous and graphic description of the outbreak of industrial warfare, but, in the end, he rolls the clouds by most conveniently, and leaves his community in the happiest of circumstances.

Terre du Ciel is a characteristic novel of his later manner in its combination of scrupulous realism in the portrayal of manners with a charming element of legend and folk-lore, testifying once more to his preoccupation with the spirit of the Vaudois countryside. Ever since The *Reign of the Evil One* an element of satire has been perceptible in his work, and here it peeps forth at the very basis of his story. The whole fable is essentially a legend, whether drawn from actual folk-lore or conceived out of the author's own imagination, telling how paradise seems to the rustic adventurers who suddenly find themselves in heaven, and deriving a peculiar savour from the style in which it is cast. C. F. Ramuz has always written remarkable French, compounded of archaisms, folk-speech, and the idiom of his country, which differs markedly in rhythm and phrase from that of France. *Terre du Ciel* is a typical piece of his prose, awkward and lumbering, but powerful, with the movement of bodies that have been bent over the plough and are no longer supple. It is the writing of one who seems peculiarly fitted to express the mind and interpret the imagination of the peasant, who has never been completely expressed in French literature. The *Reign of the Evil One* is a rural fantasia comparable to Synge's *Playboy of the Western World.* I hope in its English form it may be the means of bringing a new public to the work of the greatest Swiss novelist, who is, at the same time, one of the most original writers in the French language now living.

Ernest Boyd
New York, August, 1922.

◊

The man came about seven o'clock. It was summer, and therefore still broad daylight. He was a little thin man, limping slightly, and carrying a coarse grey canvas bag upon his back.

His arrival caused no comment among the women chatting in the village street, and the men who were busy in gardens or barns scarcely looked up from their work. Just a stray labourer, looking for a job. They were to be seen every day. One would be carrying a scythe with his bundle attached to its handle; another would have just a bundle slung about his neck. Old or young; tall, short or middling; thin or fat; whatever they were or wherever they came from, one knew they weren't worth much. Always the same bad lot: heavy drinkers, lazy, quarrelsome, difficult to get on with, and generally unsatisfactory—the shame of honest, hard-working people. He was just another of them, that was all.

The sun was reddening now, and a peaceful glow was upon the village; contentment filled every heart. Except for the fact that the dry weather seemed to be set, the year promised to be a good one: the vines below were coming on well, there had been plenty of grass for the beasts and a fine hay harvest as well. As to the corn, now just beginning to change colour, seldom had any been seen so well formed, so heavy with grain and with such fine strong stalks. These were reasons to rejoice, weren't they? Still it was not a good thing to be too cocksure, but the opposite would be worse, for to be always doubting was a gloomy business.

Men came back from the fields together, smoking pipes and shouting jokes to each other across the hedges, while bursts of gay laughter came from the women gathered round the drinking-fountain.

Little clouds floated across the evening sky; one hundred and fifty or perhaps two hundred houses pressed closely about the square-towered church, in a sort of landing on the mountain-side. Seven or eight hundred people; rather high up, if you like, but well sheltered from the north and south winds, for there were two parallel ranges between whose protecting arms stretched a peaceful valley. Each village therein had its president, three or four municipal guards, a district council with a secretary, a schoolmaster, and a priest. There were shops and an Inn, and, in front of the church, an open square where the men collected after Mass on Sundays.

Smoke rose from all the chimneys, and a rosy light gleamed upon the rocks along the mountain ridge above, so that one knew the dinner hour was not far off. And there were other signs of the approaching meal. All the roads leading in from the fields were full of people and mules; the joy of living over-flowed in this radiant hour, and even the wooden fences around the little gardens seemed to come to life. The smell of dinner came out of opened doors, and women bent over their fires within.

The man entered the Inn. It was empty, and he sat down at one of the tables at the far end of the big room. He put his canvas bag on a bench and sat with his elbows on the table, waiting to be served. Before long Simon, the inn-keeper, appeared and asked:

"What would you like?"

"A glass of wine. And something to eat too, please."

No ceremony on the part of either; Simon went to fetch bread and cheese, which he brought back on a plate, with the glass of wine.

A big copper lamp, still unlit, hung from the ceiling, and the dusk gathered in the corners of the room. The man ate slowly, as though he had no appetite; he was obliged to eat; it was dinner-time, and nourishment was a necessity. He had a cold, and a slight cough disturbed the regular movement of his jaws under a short beard covering his cheeks and chin with hairs of equal length. One couldn't quite tell what colour his beard was. He seemed to have grey eyes, but this wasn't certain, for they were little eyes and very deep-set. It was clear that he had a crooked nose, and also that his skin fitted loosely about his face, hands, and neck, and it looked more like some kind of garment than skin—something that he could take off like a coat.

There was a kind of anxiety in his expression, but he appeared to be completely at his ease and free from shyness. In fact he was perfectly calm and acted as though he were quite sure of himself. He was one of those men who make themselves at home wherever they are, who give one the impression of having said finally, "I must be taken as I am."

He kept on drinking and eating until his glass and his plate were empty; then he filled his pipe. Outside, night had come.

At that moment Simon entered the room, and, dragging a stool from beneath one of the tables, he stood upon it and lit a match on his trousers. A tiny flame began to creep slowly round the dirty wick. Congo lamps, they were called; the villages all had them; shades of cheap white china and brass containers with holes up through them to create a draught for the flame.

"You haven't got electricity here yet?"

Simon blew upon the chimney before putting it in place again.

"No—not yet; no need of it."

"That's true," said the man. "All these inventions complicate life uselessly. Just like the railways. I like my legs better, and it doesn't cost so much."

He began to laugh, but Simon didn't, being of a distrustful nature. He was slow at making friends, especially with unknown people. Anyhow, the door opened at that moment, and three men came in. They saw that someone was there, but pretended not to, and, after greeting Simon, they sat down at a table as far away as possible from the stranger. Simon had gone to the cellar without waiting for their orders, for he knew their wants from long habit. The atmosphere was already blue and getting thicker, so that the flame of the lamp became fainter and fainter until it finally looked like a little eye. Other men had come in, and a large volume of smoke rose from pipefuls of strong, coarse tobacco from the village shops: two sous a packet, labelled with a picture of a soldier with a breast-plate, and the trade mark beneath.

Conversation soon became animated; Simon, having served the latest arrivals, joined one of the groups and drank with them. Soon it was impossible to hear single voices, and discussions passed into wrangles; every now and then fists struck the tables, and each time there followed a short period of silence, after which the noise began again.

The man profited by one of these silences:

"Excuse me, gentlemen!" and every one turned to see who had spoken. They had forgotten him, but he had the floor at once, in no way embarrassed at seeing the attention of every one fixed upon him:

"Excuse me for disturbing you, but I'd like to ask a question." One saw immediately that he was used to people; shyness was unknown to him. And his audience would have remained speechless had not Lhôte, the farrier, been there. He was, fortunately, able to express himself easily and clearly. He answered for them.

"You have only to say what it is you want and we'll try to answer you."

"Thank you," the man said. Then, after a short silence, he went on:

"This is what I have to say, and it's likely to surprise you. I've come a long way and you don't know who I am. I've been so long on the road that I don't remember all the places I've been to. And I usually leave a place very soon after getting there, but this evening, as I came up here—I don't know what it was—but I found myself saying: 'What if you stopped and rested awhile? You've been wandering about enough; you're beginning to be short of breath, and you're getting on in years. Why not settle down here?'"

He spoke carefully, choosing his words as though he were selecting pieces of money to pay a bill:

"Are you in need of a shoemaker here?"

This question took everybody by surprise, and there was a silence. How extraordinary that a mere passer-by should suddenly declare his intention of settling down to live in your village! One didn't know these people, or their fathers, or their mothers; not even their names. When one of them walked through the high street, one turned aside and spat. They passed on and one had spat, that was all. But there was something about this man that his predecessors had lacked. "Why not?" they thought. "Why not, after all?" And they looked at each other while they waited for Lhôte to speak.

If he had followed his habit, Lhôte would undoubtedly have said—"You'd better go your way." But he said just the contrary.

"It's strange how things fall out. We might have sent for you, your arrival is so well-planned. Old Porte died only three days ago; he was buried yesterday. And we were anxious to know who was going to fill his place. He was a shoemaker like yourself and his shop is vacant now. "Only" (here Lhôte seemed to hesitate), "only, a sum of money would be...oh, not very much...but at least fifty francs; you see, there are his tools and some back rent to pay."

The man said: "That's my look-out..."

Then he was silent a moment, but went on in a low voice as though talking to himself: "I know it will cost something; I've thought of that; I've got..."

Then he spoke aloud:

"And when can I see the house?"

"Tomorrow morning," Lhôte said.

And the rest joined in:

"Yes, tomorrow morning."

Everybody spoke at once; they had now lost their shyness and mistrust:

"And it's a good shop too," said one, "and a fine location..."

"And a nice lot of customers, too," said another.

"And you've got to be rich," said a third, "for you have to pay cash."

"Thank you, gentlemen!" He touched the brim of his hat. "And thanks especially, you over there with the black beard," he pointed to Lhôte.

"My name is Lhôte. I'm the blacksmith." "Well, Mr. Lhôte..." and he tapped the table with the bottom of his glass—" I say, Mr. Innkeeper..."

How was it that the atmosphere had changed so quickly? One could see what they thought of the man already by the speed with which Simon came at his call.

"Three litres for these gentlemen, and of your best!"

That was the grand climax—three litres! No one was prepared for it; in fact so great was their surprise that no one dreamed of saying thanks, not even Lhôte. Could they have mistaken his words? Three litres! There were only eight people, and they had done nothing yet! Was he rich or merely generous? Anyhow they didn't waste much time pondering that, and when the Inn-keeper returned with the three litres they found words. They all spoke at once. Some: "Ah, thanks!" Others: "That's fine!" And Lhôte once more voiced sentiments that every one subscribed to:

"We aren't very good at expressing ourselves, but we are delighted to have you drinking with us."

As he said this he turned to his friends and they all took, up his phrase:

"That's it, come along, we'll be delighted!"

The man didn't hesitate: "The pleasure is mine," he said, as he rose from his chair and sat down next to Lhôte. So they pressed in closely around one table; it is always pleasant to touch elbows during certain moments of expansion.

Glasses were refilled and the talk was general—they were ten, counting the Inn-keeper, and they soon began to feel warm from the wine, a delicious melting warmth—a ray of winter sum falling on frozen ground. The man began to speak of the country round about and of how he had liked it at once, and his companions' pride was tickled. Of course they all complained of it bitterly among themselves, but just the same deep in their hearts they loved it because it was their own. There was love in their hatred of it; none of them ever left it unless obliged to, and then only with the idea of returning at the earliest opportunity.

"Then it's true that you like it here?

We shall be glad to have you with us."

Then the man asked further questions:

"How many people?"

"Seven or eight hundred."

"What trades?"

"Hardly any. We're all peasants here."

Who was the priest, who the President of the Parish, and so on? They were kept busy answering. Then the inevitable second phase of coarse stories set in and it was soon ten o'clock.

The man asked if he could have a room for the night; Simon told him there was one and went off to make the bed. While he was upstairs Lhôte asked the question that had long been on the tip of his tongue: "Excuse the indiscretion, but we'd all like to know who it is who's given us this pleasant evening, for it has been pleasant, really; I'm not just talking."

"If I rightly understand you, it's my name you'd like to know?" the man said.

"If it wouldn't be indiscreet."

"My father's name was Branchu; an easy one to remember... Branchu, as you would say Cornu."

It was indeed an easy name to remember, though it was an unusual one.

◊◊

They met by arrangement the following morning, and the affair went off without difficulty. The house was in a little street, leading away from the church, that followed a wide semi-circle to the north and rejoined the high street that cut the village in two. It had only one floor and looked like a cube of stone.

Lhôte met Branchu and they knocked at a door nearby, where the old man lived who owned the late shoemaker's dwelling. He soon stuck his head out and looked at Branchu, coughing violently.

"So it's you wanting to rent it! What a time I had with the last tenant!" Complaints began to pour forth. Porte was drinking up all his earnings, and the trouble was that when he came home drunk he made such a noise with his sighing and groaning that everybody in the village knew what had happened. He used to go on like this:

"Porte, Porte, confound you; there's a poison in you that's eating up everything, you can't enjoy yourself anymore and you are hunting pleasure through drink, but you can't see that you'll soon be beyond pleasure and there'll be nothing left but trouble. Poor old Porte, you're being poisoned. You must stop the drink, but you haven't got the strength to do it. Oh, dear! Oh, dear!..."

He used to go on like this for hours, and then he sighed and beat his chest. No one could close an eye. His death was a relief to everyone.

"So you see," continued the garrulous old man, "what I want this time is a peaceful tenant. And another thing is that Porte owed me three months' rent... And then" (here he tilted his head a little) "I would like to have a year's rent in advance; otherwise I'll keep the house empty. That would be a hundred francs for the year, and then the twenty-five francs back rent. A hundred and then twenty-five; that would be a hundred and twenty-five..." He had begun to stutter.

Branchu was splendid. The rent was being doubled, for Porte had paid only five francs a month. He took out his wallet and drew from it three notes. "There's a hundred and fifty francs." The old man stretched out his hand, then withdrew it again, and one saw that it trembled; money was scarce, and these notes with figures engraved on them were hardly ever seen. The old man held out his hand again, and again withdrew it. But Branchu said:

"Wait a moment! You can tell by looking at me that I'll be a quiet tenant."

This time the old fellow made up his mind. He took the three notes, counted them three times, folded them in half and put them in his pocket. Then he said regretfully:

"Then I owe you....I owe you twenty-five francs."

But Branchu replied—"Keep it!"

Of course in such circumstances the business went off without a hitch; the key was produced immediately and the door was opened for Branchu. The landlord hurried in past him to open the shutters:

"There you are, and it's all yours. I hope you'll be comfortable; it's just the place for you, and there's no better location for a man in your trade." Comfortable was hardly the word: a biggish room in front and a tiny one behind it. Porte might at least have left his mattress and his tools behind him, but there was no sign of either. Complete emptiness except for some useless objects: a broken packing case, some bottles and bits of leather, a brimless hat, an old pair of braces, and a terrific smell. Lhôte was a little ashamed, but Branchu did not seem in the least disappointed.

"Just what I wanted," he said. The proprietor was relieved: "It's still in rather a mess; all it needs is a good sweeping out."

This was all that happened; Branchu took Lhôte for a drink, and then set out in search of a mason. He did the sweeping-up himself with a broom borrowed from the proprietor. The latter offered his help in the operation, but Branchu refused it, and the mason soon arrived. He distempered the walls within and without, and gave the front door and the two ceilings a coat of paint. Upon the mud floors he laid down a thin layer of cement.

But the wonder of wonders was to come a few days later, on Saturday afternoon. The villagers walked past to see what he was doing to the house, and they saw a beautiful, freshly-painted sign fixed to the wall above the window—yellow letters on a blue background:

BRANCHU, Shoemaker

To the left a woman's shoe with a red top, and at the right a man's black shoe with a tree inside it. The villagers' admiration was unbounded; never before had they beheld such a splendid sign in the village. Branchu must have painted it himself, and secretly, too, for no one had seen him doing it. Undoubtedly he had a weakness for surprising people. What an extraordinary fellow, and where on earth had he gotten all that money!

These things were being discussed when Branchu appeared in front of the inn. He was still lodging there, for the carpenter from whom he had ordered his furniture had not yet finished it. Some of the people started to move away when they saw that he was coming towards them; others pretended not to see him, but several stepped forward to meet him. He held out his hand, and when they had congratulated him he said:

"I thought a long time about the colour. Perhaps it would have been better to have a red background—flame-colour is my favourite shade."

For the first time, he laughed.

◊◊◊

Some days later the carpenter delivered the furniture. On Monday morning Branchu went away, and no one saw him go. The following Saturday he returned bringing another man who led a mule by the bridle. The beast was covered with sweat, and its bit was white with foam.

Branchu helped the man to unload parcels from the pack-saddle. First came two big bags, then a flat leather saddle-bag that must have contained bits of iron, to judge by the noise it made. Everything was taken into the front room where a bench had already been put up, and Branchu (he was known to everybody by this name now) paid the man with the mule 15 francs and 30 centimes, whereupon he departed; not, however, until he had stopped for a drink at the Inn and told of his having come from Borne-Dessous, a little town in the valley. And he did not conceal the fact that his mule had that day carried a supply of all kinds of leather and every sort of thing needed by a shoemaker establishing himself in his trade.

The truth of his remarks was evident the following day when Branchu opened his shop to the public. Skins hung from all the walls, and rows of new tools shone from the bench: hammers, paring-knives, and awls, a pot of wax, and boxes of nails and pegs. The shoemaker himself was sitting on a low chair without a back, tapping upon the little round-ended anvil that he had fixed before him.

The sun had just appeared above the mountain top; the day would be a perfect one. Little round clouds came up over the ridge and sailed higher, leaving the sun behind them. Most people would have shaded their eyes against the light, but it made no difference to Branchu. His clothes were all new: a fine new green canvas apron and a striped flannel shirt with the cuffs turned up. There he was, a first rate shoemaker, in good spirits; not very young, but what difference did that make? And after all not very old either. He looked in the best of health and seemed keen about his job. People passing by thought: "Such a relief after old Porte! What a dreadful old thing he was!"

The little street was one of the most used in the village; men, women, and children passed through it continually, and by the time twelve o'clock had struck, there was no one who did not know that Branchu had begun to work.

Four or five days went by before any business came his way. They wanted to see what he could do, and the backing of public opinion was necessary for even the tiniest order. Shall we call it prudence? And so it was that Branchu had plenty of time to make a fine pair of lady's shoes with varnished flaps, which he hung just inside the window. These were the envy of all the girls who saw them, but they remained on the hook in the window frame until Lhôte came one morning with a pair of his own shoes, saying: "These must be re-soled."

He was the first customer (politeness had brought him), but he had no cause for regret. Before evening his shoes were ready. He asked what he owed. Two francs. It was just half what he was used to paying, and he hurried anxiously away in order to examine the work carefully. The leather was of the finest quality, and he could hardly believe his eyes. And when he put the shoes on they were even more comfortable than before. It was astonishing to have paid so little and got such good value! A pair of shoes he had worn for four years, and now they looked like new ones; and they shone so brightly with the waxing they had been given that he could hardly look at them. He wondered what sort of wax had been used.

A customer's advertisement is the best, clearly, and the following morning many followed Lhôte's example. Before the end of the week the shoes with varnished flaps no longer hung inside the window. It was Virginie Poudret who had bought them; the desire to make others jealous was strong in her and it would soon be Sunday.

"It will be better for no one to know," she said to herself.

"My friends haven't the courage—well, I have, that's all, and the man won't eat me."

She went to the shop about noon when there was no one in the streets…

"How much are they?" repeated Branchu. "Have you looked at me. Mademoiselle?" Then he went on: "I'm not a Jew. And when one is as pretty as you are…I'll make you a present of them."

Virginie got very red, but there they were being held out to her; she had to take them. Branchu wanted to try them on her himself, and he knelt before her to remove her slippers. And what poor shabby old things they were! Stained brown with dew and grey with dust, and a string for lacing. What a change for Virginie! The new shoes fitted her perfectly; as Branchu said, they might have been made for her.

When she got home with her parcel under her arm, she seemed oddly enough to have acquired an added self-respect. She felt proud of herself, but she spoke of the shoes to no one. On Sunday she went to Mass with the other girls, but no one had the faintest idea what had occurred until afterwards when they all went out into the square and gathered beneath an old lime-tree (said to be three hundred years old) which offered a pleasant escape from the hot sun. It was there that the full glory of Virginie's new shoes burst upon her friends. She had only to lift her skirt, and they all turned to gaze and exclaim:

"Will you look at that!"

"It's not possible!"

"Does she imagine she's pretty?"

"It's a pity her face doesn't match her feet!" And they laughed at her, but you felt it was hollow laughter. Some were so angry that they shrugged their shoulders and looked away, but most of them being more curious than jealous began to ask questions:

"How much did you pay? Tell us."

"Are they the ones we saw hanging in the window?"

"What pretty feet they give you!"

"Aren't they too small?"

"Don't they hurt just a tiny bit?"

While Virginie was satisfying her questioners, Lhôte was drawing admiration from another group.

"Two francs, I said; not a sou more!"

It was easy to guess from this that it did not take Branchu many days to establish himself; he soon had more work than three ordinary shoemakers could handle. How on earth did he manage it? But he did, though to most people it seemed an impossibility. No one could find the slightest ground for complaint. Always the same ridiculous prices.

"Naturally," they said, "he makes up on the quantity of work, but how quickly he must have to work!" He soon became the admiration of all; it was splendid of him, and most people knew how to appreciate good workmanship.

Branchu, on his side, knew how to make friends; hardly a week passed without his taking one or two of his customers for a drink at the Inn. Free drinks never go unappreciated. Also he knew that it would never do, in the long run, to expect people to be satisfied if he divulged no details of his past life, so he set about telling his story little by little: He was born of parents he had never known, far away somewhere down the valley. He was brought up by some wicked people who had made him sleep on a pile of shavings. One day when he could endure his life with them no longer, he ran away; then his wandering had begun. When he earned a franc, he bought things here and there that he could sell for one franc twenty, and after a while he found he had saved up a tidy little sum. But he had earned it well, and honestly too, because this wandering life of his was a very hard one; "and my feet are worn away from walking," he said, "a good half inch all round, as though someone had sand-papered them."

It wasn't surprising that he finally came to the end of his wanderings, and "here, I'm quite happy because I am among friends."

"That's true!" And then someone asked:

"Where did you learn your shoemaking?"

"Ah, yes," he said. "I forgot to tell you that. It was in Germany."

"In Germany!"

◊◊◊◊

There was one man in the village who kept saying:

"Be on your guard!"

It is true that this man, Luc, had always been considered off his head. Sometimes he pretended to see the Virgin or one of the Saints, and often it was Jesus himself who appeared to him. He had studied for the priesthood, then he had tried to make himself a notary, but he never got to be a priest or a notary; no one had ever known him to be anything. His sister took him in to live with her, else he would have died of hunger. He spent days on end reading ponderous books, and when he was not reading he walked the streets, stopping in front of people's houses to remind them of the Commandments. His big, tangled beard seemed to spring out just beneath a shabby bowler hat, drawn down to his ears, and his long-tailed coat was worn and frayed at the edges. The children in the streets threw stones at him, but he only turned and shook his fist at them. There are many men like him—men who, finding nothing to do in life, give themselves up to dreaming. They seldom face actualities and they keep muttering strange phrases and making crazy gestures. They do not frighten any one, and they end by not even causing surprise. The only purpose they serve is to make people laugh.

So it was that when Luc began to attack Branchu, people simply shrugged their shoulders and told him to go away. But it only made him talk louder.

Now there was another shoemaker in the village, named Jacques Musy; he was always ill, poor fellow, and it made him melancholy. His cheeks had fallen in, and he was hollow-chested, and sometimes his shop was closed for several days running because he could not work. Naturally there were times when you had to wait a long time for work to be done, but he had never been in want of it because people pitied him. Still, pity with most people is a Sunday affair; it is like a fine suit of clothes not worn every day. When Branchu became known as a clever and a cheap shoemaker, Jacques Musy was abandoned. It was no use his remaining in his shop, seated on his low work-chair, for he saw clearly what it was that threatened him. No one ever came to him now. He looked out of his window; some little girls were playing "Heaven and Hell" with a flat stone which they kicked about upon a design of squares marked on the earth with a stick. The clock struck—in an hour it struck again; not a single pair of slippers to mend, and when he thought of the row of them there used to be on his bench...! For a fortnight he was patient, even for three weeks; and then people began to wonder how he kept alive.

One fine morning he did not open his shop, and no one thought anything of it; no doubt he was ill. Two or three days passed like this, and it was only by chance that a neighbour found his body on the fourth morning hanging from the back of his front door. There was a horrible smell and his face was quite black.

No bells were rung for him, and he was buried in a corner like an animal. People would soon have forgotten him and the way he died (such things happened too often), if Luc had not taken this opportunity to shout louder than ever in the streets:

"Now, you see!"

"What do we see?" they said to him.

"Whether I was wrong or not, when I told you to be on your guard. There you are, Jacques Musy is dead!"

"He is. And what of it? The good fortune of some is the misfortune of others. It's always like that and always will be."

That was one way of looking at things, and perhaps it was the wisest, but Luc shouted just as loudly as before, wandering the streets and shaking his head.

CHAPTER II

◊

It was at least three or four months after Branchu had installed himself in the village that signs began to be apparent. One October morning Baptiste's gun went off in his hands, while he was out after rabbits. He sat on a pile of faggots in front of his cottage and some women went to fetch a pail of water; in a jiffy the water was red, and when he saw his blood flowing into it he was sick at his stomach.

"Heavens," the women said, "he is getting it badly!" And all the time the heart-pump inside him sent forth a thin jet which could not be stopped until a thick layer of cobweb was applied to the wound.

Three days later, a man called Mudry, Baptiste's cousin, fell almost a hundred yards from the top of a cliff and split his head in two. And little Louise, the bell-ringer's daughter, got the croup. Two beasts died that same night in the same cattle-shed; and a brand new loft of hay was destroyed by fire.

All those things were or might have been coincidences; there is a proverb that says, "Misfortunes never come singly." But much the most disquieting thing of all was the change in the people themselves; they were changing rapidly, and for the worse.

There was, for instance, Trente-et-Quarante, who had had a child of a woman not his wife. He was too poor to pay the baby's keep, and as he no longer cared for its mother, he put it in a bag one evening when she had left it asleep and had gone to fetch water from the fountain. He carried the bag down into the valley, tied a big stone to it, and threw it into the river. He watched it sinking and was happy at what he had done.

Then there was that fight among the village boys one night as they came from the vineyards. A troop of them were climbing up to the village—a little drunk it must be admitted, but, though new wine is always tricky, it wasn't possible to blame it all on that. So far as one could tell from the accounts of it later, the trouble was about a girl; one of them boasted of having kissed her when he had not. Therefore what was there to boast of? It is all very well to pull a person's leg but it must stop if taken too seriously. Bernard did just the opposite, and the other chap, Jean, who really cared for the girl, could not bear it.

"Chuck it, or I'll…"

"You'll what?" asked Bernard.

There were fifteen of them, and it was pitch dark on the last grassy short-cut into the village. Two voices came up through the stillness, and then the two combatants made for each other. The others, instead of trying to separate them as they should have done, divided into two shouting bands of supporters. "At him, Bernard!" "At him, Jean!" But neither of them needed the slightest encouragement, for they were both furious.

Three times they rose up and three times they went down again; the moon sailed clear of the clouds. Moon, you are witness; it was night and they were coming back from the vineyards with too much new wine in them, but that doesn't explain why those two lay there on the ground, the one on the top pounding the face of the one beneath him. And even now, does one understand why it happened…? Those two were not the only ones fighting. The rest of them soon joined in, and their shouts brought people to the windows. Men came out with lanterns saying, "What's going on?" And when they saw that the moon was shining: "Good Heavens, look up there!" And the women: "Oh, dear—oh, dear!" Women, children in their nightclothes;

how cold it was standing there with the north wind blowing down from the mountain!

Some of the men went bravely forward with sticks and tried to put an end to the combat, but they had to wait for it to peter out for lack of fighters.

Four of the boys lay motionless on the ground, and in the morning the puddles of blood had not dried up; for a long time a kind of brown crust was to be seen there, but the wind blew it away in flakes, little by little, until there was none of it left.

As for Jean he was in bed for six weeks. It was astonishing that he, the one who had really been in the right, had had so much the worst of it; Bernard escaped without injury. Jean's jaw was broken, his, forehead cut open, one ankle sprained, and he had wounds all over his body. A high fever came soon, and he had to be carefully nursed; the doctor who was called in said at first that his skull had been fractured, and for a while they thought he would not recover.

And all this time Bernard swaggered about the village, saying: "He knows what I am now; he won't come meddling in my affairs anymore." And he laughed as he walked about the streets holding his nose high in the air. Then the expected happened; he took Jean's sweetheart from him without really intending to. She simply came up to him one day, and putting her arms about his neck, said: "I love you because you're the strongest."

That seemed hardly fair, but she ended by having to leave that part of the country.

Clinche's household came next. He had always been a most reasonable and sweet-natured man; his wife was a good woman and the children were well behaved and their bringing-up had been quite easy. Suddenly a change came over Clinche, and every evening when he came in, he was full of hard words and reproaches. First it was the soup, too cold or too hot; then there was a smell in the kitchen and it made him cough. Sometimes he complained that everything was in a mess, and if all was tidy he told his wife she was wasting her time. He was always on the look-out for something to quarrel about, and, alas, it soon came to beating.

At first she said nothing to his accusations, for she was mystified by his treatment of her, and her sweetness and easy obedience prevented her from replying. She well knew that men sometimes changed and therefore she was patient. But her patience was of no avail, and he became fussier and more brutal as time went on.

"Oh, Jean," she said one day, unable to keep silence longer—"how can you forget everything? Don't you remember the time when you came to me first? You didn't use such hard words then! It was I who said no, but when you wept at night beneath my window, I pitied you... And now you don't want me any longer..."

"Leave me alone," he said. "See how much time you're wasting. Get that broom, I tell you—quicker than that—or else I'll..."

He lifted his fist and the children started to cry.

It was Hell in that house; you could hear little Henri pleading with his father—"Papa, please, please don't hit me." Clinche paid no heed to the little boy's entreaties, and beat him as he had beaten his wife, and the whole village would have heard his cries if the wind had not blown them away, down into the valley. Then the wind fell and the tiny voice rose out of the silence and the shadows, to die away. Little by little in a long moan like the wind itself coming in through a crack in the wall.

◊◊

Lude went out that same evening without knowing why, or where he wanted to go. The desire to walk somewhere had taken possession of him. His wife asked if he would be back soon, and he answered:

"Mind your own business!"

She was astonished at those words, for her husband loved her. But in this household, too, a change had come. Something unusual was going on in Lude's mind, and even he did not know what it was. He was conscious of an inner burden of uneasiness that he wanted to get rid of, that obliged him to set forth that evening like a beast whose pack is too heavy and who wants to drop it by the roadside. Since the day before, the sky had been overcast; it was only a change in the direction of the wind—a small matter, but it gave everything a different aspect. Golden-yellow leaves were no more, and the trees stretched out bare arms against the greyness. The close-cropped grass had lost its brilliance and the sky rested heavily upon the mountains. Life seemed as difficult for people as for things. Jean Lude felt this, and he wondered how he had been able to endure such a life of misery. As a matter of fact, one might say he had never suffered at all till now; few people had had such happiness, and he was always pointed out as the model husband of the parish. He was tall and thin, and he had a long neck with a very prominent Adam's apple. His features betrayed a charming disposition and he had the look of a person who accepts life as it is.

Now he accepted it no longer. He swallowed hard and his Adam's apple rose up towards his chin. His mouth was dry, as though he were sickening, and he wondered what could be the matter with him, but no solution offered itself, and he climbed farther up the mountain side. The road split in two at a little plateau, and he stood for a moment looking, down towards the village. A thick mist, like a covering of white linen, had hidden everything down there except the church tower, which was sticking up through a tear in it. When the wind blew, a slight movement could be seen like a wavelet passing over a lake, and every now and then a fragment detached itself and was blown slowly up towards him—he thought of an old man sitting close to a wall smoking a pipe—the first puff glided horizontally away beneath him, then a second came nearer, followed by many others in quick succession.

He had seen the mist rise like that often enough, but when the obscurity folded him in he felt lonely, being cut off from his fellow men, quite alone at the fall of night, up there at the forking roads.

One of them led higher up the mountain; the other went along upon the same level, and after hesitating a moment he took the level road, but he did not know yet what his destination was to be. He felt he had to keep moving; he had stopped just now because he had felt like stopping. Now he was walking again. Finally, he came to a place called Prézimes, but he kept thinking the same thoughts: fourteen hours of work in summer, six hours of sleep; nothing but soup with bread in it, one room for the three of us; is that fair? Other people have all they want; we have nothing. When they want a new suit of clothes they have only to open their purses; we have to wear the same clothes all our lives, and even after life, for we are buried in them.

"God!" He raised a clenched fist above his head.

He stopped again and found himself exactly opposite one of his own fields; it sank away from the road that formed its upper boundary and seemed to be stitched on to the slope. There were no trees in the fields, nor bushes, nor even a ditch to show the divisions; only three or four pointed stones on end to mark out the bits of worked land in more or less equal parts.

He stared fixedly, but he was not really looking at anything; he was searching his mind for a solution, and suddenly it came:

"I would only have to move those stones a little and my troubles would be over." Five or six square feet more isn't much, but it would be a beginning and that was what he wanted. Not to be poor any longer. So much the worse if he went about it dishonestly. Of what use to be stupid; much more sensible to be clever!

He looked all about him again; then he went down into the field and took hold of the first stone he came to. A crow cawed over his head, and far away he heard the wheels of a farm-wagon creaking...

It was dark when he got home and his wife was preparing dinner. He kissed her and seemed like the old Jean Lude again. When his little girl came up to him, he said:

"Come along, Marie," and he took her upon his lap. "Do you love your daddy?"

"Oh, yes!" she said eagerly.

It was pleasantly warm in the kitchen. How cosy to be in a comfortable room with the night and a high wind outside! One sat beneath the rows of sausages in the wide chimney corner. Quarters of bacon hung there too, for the pig had just been killed.

"Food is there," he said to himself. "This is my home, and here is my wife, and my little girl."

The warmth began to do its work and he felt as though his heart were resting in cotton—like a bird that has come back to its nest in bad weather—he wanted nothing more.

Dinner was soon ready, and his appetite was better than it had been for days.

Adele went off to put little Marie to bed, then she came back and Lude made her sit down near him. Her eyes shone now with the joy and wellbeing that had come to her again.

"Ah, you bashful little thing, come closer so I can kiss you on the neck where you like it. Pretty, too, what? after the twelve years we've been married!"

Then again:

"Oh, well, come along anyway."

She only had to move a little closer...

He was silent for a long time and then, suddenly:

"Listen, what would you say if we got rich?"

She sat up quickly.

"Aren't you going to say anything?"

"I don't understand."

"What? You don't understand? I asked if you would be glad if we got rich. There's a chance for it." (He struck the table with his fist.) "It's no more than our rights. We've been poor long enough; it's our turn now."

Again Adele was afraid.

◊◊◊

Many women were now being taken with epilepsy—suddenly in the streets they fell backwards, a, kind of foam appeared at their mouths, and their faces turned deathly pale.

One could hardly help noticing that a great number of misfortunes were occurring all at once, and when people began to hunt for the cause of them there were many differences of opinion: some blamed it on the air; others said something had gone wrong with the water, still others that it was the changing season. There were a few who maintained it was only an acute epidemic of influenza, and Luc was alone in his explanation—always the same one:

"He's got a treacherous face, and there's something deceitful about the swiftness of his hands!"

He continued to walk through the streets shouting these words at the top of his voice; people became excited by his cries, but no one thought of blaming the new shoemaker. On the contrary, his shop was never empty; it was pleasant to go in there and chat with him. He always had some tale to tell you or would listen to yours. There were always at least five or six people in the shop, while he pounded a piece of leather or drew waxed thread through it, completely oblivious of the talk that was going the rounds about him. His face always wore a look of alertness; his little grey eyes shone and his tongue kept pace with those clever hands, and the amount of work that he got through in a few hours was positively incredible. He knew so well how to amuse people that they almost forgot he was there. And then suddenly Luc's voice could be heard outside, faintly at first as though stifled, but gradually gaining in volume. The words could be distinguished now: "Blind fools; curses and disaster upon you!" and the rest of it. It was impossible not to listen, and some lost their patience: "God, if that stupid old idiot would only keep still!"

Branchu was the only one who paid no attention. His little hammer with its rounded end kept on tapping:

"What can he matter to you?" he said. "Why do his words trouble you?"

He placed a finger upon his forehead: "He's nothing but a poor wretch out of his senses."

"Of course," they answered; "he doesn't bother us, but you…"

"Oh, me..." Branchu shrugged his shoulders and took up his work again. Luc appeared, at this moment, and no one could say he was a coward. They were eight and he one, but he stood there in front of the shop, his head thrown back, his beard sticking out towards them, and fire darting from his eyes.

"Have you no shame, you in there? The others are simply deaf and blind. But you can hear and see... You're traitors, I tell you; cowards...deliberately planning your own destruction!"

His voice grew louder but came to a sudden stop. Someone had just opened a window—a huge stone fell into the gutter. Luc hurried away covered with mud, and laughter filled the shop. Branchu laughed too, but his laughter was spontaneous.

A few mornings later, about eleven o'clock, Lhôte came down the street towards his house and saw some people gathered on the landing at his door—women gesturing and talking. As he drew near they fell silent, and one of them ran towards him:

"Lhôte, Lhôte, don't come any nearer; don't, it's too sad." She stretched out her hands trying to stop him. "Leave us to take care of her; you wait till she's better! If you don't—if you don't..."

He pushed her aside roughly and ran up the steps to the landing. Inside he found his mother lying motionless upon the kitchen table. She was not dead, for it was evident that she could see; perhaps she saw and heard everything. But she made no movement whatever. Her brain was buried alive in the tomb of her body.

Lhôte fell upon his knees beside her:

"Mother," he cried, "Mother! Don't you hear? It's me." He spoke like a little child. He rose up and bent over her, but she did not move, nor did her eyes turn towards him. She was like one of those images that lie upon the flagstones of a church, except that her heart was beating. And what grief in that heart if she could hear her son calling her!

The women who had crowded into the kitchen whispered to each other: "Nobody can do anything. It's total paralysis!"

This is common enough among old people when they come to the end of their strength; something snaps inside, and everyone knows there is no doctor who can cure an illness like that. It is something beyond the reach of human power. So when Lhôte suggested sending for the doctor the women shook their heads, and one of them said:

"My poor Lhôte, really, the doctor can't do anything, and you'll have to pay at least twenty francs."

He evidently saw that they were right and gave up the idea. Then, drawing a stool close to the table, he sat upon it and crossed his arms. His mother still lay motionless; her old face was like carved wood, her lips were drawn, and her big crooked nose rose up between two sunken eyes. Someone had put a plaid covered cushion beneath her white capped head. She seemed to have stopped breathing, so slight was the rise and fall of her breast, and one wondered whether her heart could really be beating, and if it were beating, how long it would last.

People came in to look and went out again. Some spoke a word or two, others were silent, but nothing seemed to matter, and Lhôte sat upon his stool without moving. A long time passed like this; night began to fall, and people in wooden-soled shoes kept clacking up the stone steps and pushing open the door. Outside there was just enough light to see that it was snowing a little. In the low-ceilinged room there was an overwhelming smell of wet clothes.

At the stroke of four the door opened again and Branchu came in. No one was surprised to see him, for his friendship with Lhôte was well known, and they stood back to let him pass. He went up to the table where the old woman lay and put his hand upon his friend's shoulder. Lhôte looked up at him with troubled eyes that seemed to ask what was expected of him.

"Lhôte," said Branchu, "don't you know me?"

He nodded and then let his head fall back upon his breast. Then Branchu turned to the old woman; he took her hand and lifted it up and held it for a moment without speaking, lost in thought. When his voice broke the stillness again, hardly anyone recognised it.

"Lhôte, what would you say if I cured her?"

Lhôte still did not reply, but his eyes never left those of Branchu who now moved even closer to the table. He stretched out his arms, opened his hands wide and slowly lowered them until they rested upon the old woman's breast. He moved them to the right and to the left, barely touching at first, then pressing more and more. They went all over her body, rising and falling, now resting over her heart, now gliding from her neck to her cheeks and forehead. Suddenly he bent forward, weighing down with his hands; they saw his chest sink and then his breath escaped with a rush.

"There—it wasn't so hard to do!" he said, and then for the second time he broke into a fit of laughter (he had laughed like this before when telling the first visitor to his shop that he wished he had used red paint for his sign), and the tension in the room was broken.

Every one pushed forward, and, in the centre of the circle, they saw old Marguerite's face beginning to change colour. Her eyes moved, and her hands groped weakly for her skirt. She seemed to be trying to speak, for her lips were moving. Suddenly the words came:

"Where am I?"

She was trying to sit up.

"Can this be possible?" cried the people encircling her. "She has come back! Lhôte, don't you hear? She has spoken!"

Lhôte alone seemed to have heard nothing; they helped him to stand up, and mother and son looked at one another. A smile fluttered over the old toothless mouth like a butterfly preparing to settle, and then she stretched out her arms to him. Lhôte now understood what had happened. No one could doubt it any longer. She was cured. Her arms were about his neck:

"Is it you? Is it really you?"

Tongues were loosed, and the women nearest all spoke at once, telling her what had occurred:

"You fell and we came and lifted you on to the table. You lay there as though dead. And it's a good thing Branchu..."

They would have gone on to say that he had only had to... But Lhôte stood up and raising his hand: "I know who he is! He's Jesus!"

The door flew open and struck against the wall. Too many people; the room wouldn't hold them. Nevertheless they crowded in; curiosity had to be satisfied. Every one shouted, "Is it true?" and the old woman answered, "You can see for yourselves."

She seemed absolutely herself now and perfectly happy, looking even younger than before. Her colour was better and her eyes had a new brightness. Someone brought her a cup of coffee, and she drank it sitting in an old wicker chair by the fire; she was surrounded by her friends, who told the whole story, with suitable gestures, to each newcomer. And so it happened that Lhôte was forgotten for a moment. Branchu had been gone a long time.

Then suddenly Lhôte's voice rose above the others in the gathering darkness; it had a hollow sound, for he had long been deep in thought: "Jesus has come back to us!"

Someone stood up on a bench to light the lamp, and Lhôte came forward to the middle of the room:

"Do you all realise what has happened? Our troubles will soon be over!" His pale face beneath his black beard made them wonder whether he could be the man they had once known—a jovial fellow standing in his leather apron, while he drew smoke from a mule's hoof and exchanged jokes with the man who held its head.

He raised his hand again: "Listen to me! I tell you that Christ is among us. He was a carpenter; he's a shoemaker now, but it doesn't matter if his trade has changed. We know who he is because he cures the sick and causes the dead to stand up in their grave clothes."

Many of his listeners were inclined to think as he did; others could not bring themselves to believe it. But, after all, it was difficult to deny that they had witnessed a miracle. What if there were going to be others!

So many people entered the open door that one hardly knew where they could have come from. Then they all went out into the night because Lhôte went out. Even some sick people were there, and they knew the star that drew them, for Lhôte walked in front. "Perhaps," they said to themselves, "but is one ever sure of anything?" There is always, within, a great desire to believe, and Lhôte was leading the way.

He turned to the left at the first corner. It was still snowing a little—tiny flakes that seemed to come not only from the sky, but from everywhere. The wind blew softly, and little cold needles melted on people's eye-lashes. No star shone in the sky, but suddenly that other bright star of the earth could be seen. It was the shop where he was—the gleam from his window. They all went towards it.

Lhôte knocked at the door; it was opened and quickly shut again. Every one pressed forward so as to see in through the window, since it was impossible to enter the house. The sick ones asked:

"Won't he cure us today? It's hard to have to wait."

Some were coughing, and one poor little boy, walking on crutches, had to sit down in the mud because he could not stand up any longer.

◊◊◊◊

Branchu's door remained closed and they could not enter. It was explained that he could only cure certain diseases. Lhôte alone had been allowed to go in.

It was almost eight o'clock and the village was generally asleep by that time. In winter there was nothing to do in the evenings, so instead of burning oil they went to bed, and silence reigned above those little roofs that clustered together sometimes in moonlight and often in mist, and there was nothing to be heard but the fountain, which sounded like tiny muffled drum-taps. But, on that evening, voices sounded faintly in the streets; some had stayed to talk in spite of the snow. Suddenly a cry rose up, and the occupants of the shop (several others had been allowed to join Lhôte) listened to these words of warning:

"Hear me before it is too late. He has played the opposite role in order to deceive you more easily. It's like putting honey on a plate for flies…"

"It's easy to say who that is," someone said, "and he must be made to hold his tongue."

"Leave that to me," Lhôte said, but Branchu held him back and the voice was soon inaudible. No doubt poor Luc was making another round of the village, stopping before the houses to cry his warning:

"It's the last chance."

An awkward silence was broken suddenly by Branchu:

"Don't let's stay here. I know what we'll do." And he took them to the Inn as he had often done before.

There was more light there and it was warmer. Wine would make conversation far easier. They sat down, and the customary atmosphere was restored again. Some people came in and asked Branchu:

"Is it true that you perform miracles?" And Branchu shrugged his shoulders.

"I, perform miracles! Alas, no, my friend; nor is there anyone in this world who can. I've learned a little medicine, and I can be of service every now and then."

Others arrived then and asked:

"Are you Jesus, or the Devil himself?"

Branchu replied laughing: "Neither Jesus nor the Devil. I'm between them." And at this Lhôte looked at him strangely.

It was easy to see that no one knew what to believe; their minds had not had time to grasp the situation. In any case they considered him now in a new light, and they respected him. The middle course was the one to follow: "he's a very wise man who's hiding his light under a bushel," and people like that were difficult to manage.

Branchu was a perfect host; never had wine flowed more freely. What was his idea? Every new arrival was given a drink at once. A comfortable warm feeling prevailed, and pipes glowed and smoke rose up. They were all his friends or friends of his friends and he seemed delighted that they were there, and endeavoured to keep them by means of a continual filling of glasses—Lhôte alone did not drink. Later on in the evening the voice was heard again outside. It grew louder and louder:

"It's the last chance to escape. The door down there is open now—he's leading you on with soft words, but I'm telling you where it is he's taking you—you can get away from him if you like…"

Some of them burst out laughing. Lhôte stood up, but Branchu signed to him to sit down again. Lhôte shook his head, saying:

"No, no! It isn't right, it isn't right. I obey because it's you, but the thing isn't right!"

"Come, come," said Branchu, "remember what I told you." Then he went on, trying to pacify the minds of his friends:

"After all, he hasn't done harm to any one; and least of all to me. Naturally for the good of the village it would be well to have him locked up, but there's no hurry."

Those were his last words, and how he managed to disappear so suddenly, no one ever knew. There was a lot of smoke in the room and several men had risen during the heat of the discussion about Luc—perhaps in the disorder Branchu had taken his chance…

Luc was now standing just outside the Inn:

"Hey, up there can you hear me? It's for you that I've come and particularly for you, Lhôte, because, though your heart is pure, it's been led astray. Listen to me: your mother would be better dead, yes, much better, Lhôte, for there is something more important than the body."

Lhôte was at the window before anyone could stop him. He leaned out:

"Say that again!"

"I will!" replied Luc.

"And what if I came out?" "I would say it just the same, for it's the truth."

Lhôte was in the street before Luc had finished his last

declaration. Every one followed, and in the darkness they could just see the two men talking down each other's throats:

"It's you who are Satan, not him!" shouted Lhôte, and a noise was heard like that of a falling body. Then Lhôte turned to the others:

"Well, you people…" They had come to see what was going to happen.

"Get hold of him by the feet," said Lhôte. Loud laughter burst forth—Lhôte alone did not join in it—and they harnessed themselves to the body like so many horses to a wagon. But the wagon was very light, for a body slips easily on melting snow.

"Where shall we go? To the fountain?" It was quite near, and beneath it was a wooden tank, broad and deep.

On the ninth day after that, pneumonia carried off the man who perhaps alone had understood what was going on. He had not been numbered among the intelligent people of the village, but it is often the eyes of others who see most clearly.

CHAPTER III

◊

The days after that were peaceful ones, because Christmas was drawing near. There was happiness in the Amphion household, and while the chimes sent forth the glad tidings, Joseph and Héloïse sat by their fire talking of the good fortune that had come to them. Héloïse's waist was certainly getting larger, and it was not surprising, for she was six months gone. Joseph could scarcely believe anything was going to happen. He had been waiting for this for three years and they had tried everything; they had even made a pilgrimage, the spring before, to Sainte-Claire.

"Ah, Héloïse, I had already begun to curse you for being barren, and, you know, if this hadn't happened I wouldn't have been able to keep on loving you. It wouldn't have been possible! Give me a kiss, quickly."

He threw a log on the fire and the flames leapt high against the chimney back, lighting up little stars of soot. She had kissed him not only once but twice, and they sat listening to the notes of the carol that poured out of the bell tower into the still night like children racing out of school.

They talked of the past three years; useless years but for the fact that they had loved each other. But when something is lacking it often seems that all is lacking. Fortunately all that was over now, otherwise their love would have come to an end.

"It's true," he said, looking into her eyes, "it did no good for me to clench my fists and throw back my head; I felt that I was giving in. It's a hard job to climb the path of discontent, but now you've pulled me up from the depths with the bigness of your waist. Another kiss!"

That one made ten, if not more.

They had often spent cosy evenings together in front of the fire—two long beech logs, with the bark on, crossed. A pleasant gleam enabled them to see each other. That was all they wanted. Another log. August, September, October, November, December. Five months...to those five months they had only to add four more: January, February, March, April. Almost a whole year; and the great moment would be when the birds began to sing and points of green appeared like little finger nails on the hedges.

Their happiness lay in the fact that they looked ahead and thus got outside themselves. They could turn their backs upon daily events, for they had so many plans and projects that they never got to the end of them. Would it, for example, be a boy or a girl?

"I naturally would rather have a boy; still, if it's a girl, I'll be quite content."

And she replied, "Whatever pleases you will be the best for me. If you are satisfied I shall be too."

They laughed then, and he said, "Is it true, Héloïse?" She threw her head back and he repeated: "Is it true, Héloïse, really...? All right, then, if it's a boy, what are we going to call him?"

"We'll have to look in the calendar."

He went to get it, and they talked of the actual date. Finally she said: "Look from the 15th to the 25th."

"The 15th," he said, "is Saint-Paterne."

"Oh, not Paterne!"

"Well, the 16th is Saint-Fructueux."

She shook her head.

"The 17th, Saint-Anicat. The 18th, Saint-Parfait. The 19th, la Quasimodo. The 20th, Saint Gaspard…" He said to himself—"Shall I go on like this all evening?" But on the 21st came Saint-Anselme.

"There," she cried,"—that's a name I like. He must be born on the 21st."

"Suits me well enough, but what if it's a girl?"

Again she was silent and could suggest nothing. He tried to think of a way out:

"We'll have to look in another Calendar. They don't all have the same Saints."

They kissed each other and laughed, and then started to talk of names again, but soon they were silent—no need to talk when she was sitting on his lap.

Happiness filled their hearts and all the rest of life seemed unimportant. The words they spoke, the little bursts of laughter, gestures, even kisses—all those were surface things. They looked beneath it all and saw a beautiful baby with a high forehead and big fat cheeks. That was the true foundation upon which they were building—the corner stone of everything. Even if he were a tiny mite, it all rested on him, and when one builds a house one must be in earnest. Suddenly Héloïse became sad; Joseph asked what was wrong; did she even know herself what these things were? A shadow had fallen across her face like a cloud over the sun.

Fortunately Joseph was beginning to recognise the little ills that come to women, so he made her go to bed. The next day, the one before Christmas, she was quite well again. They went to midnight Mass, and afterwards their relations came in to drink warmed wine, with sugar, cinnamon, cloves, and even a pinch of pepper in it.

Christmas passed and the New Year was approaching.

◊◊

At this season of the year, all the roads about these villages are impassable. The little houses are like prisons, and the mountain rises sadly into the grey sky. Of course there is Christmas Day, when a sort of light seems to descend upon everything, but when it has passed the little rooms are gloomy again and the air is heavy under the low ceilings. Outside, the mists hang low, and if a bit of fine weather comes it is soon cold and wet again. There is no work out of doors, except for those who go after wood in the forest with ropes and axes, and the best thing to do is to stay indoors and try to kill the long hours. The only regular occupation one has is to look after the animals. There are repairs to do: a new hinge for one of the shutters, a new handle for the fork or the rake; but one is always lazy about such things. What hurry is there? One wears a sweater with sleeves made of coarse brown wool; looks out of the window, sits by the fire, or tries to read a newspaper. The children cry continually during these dreary winter months, and many of them have handkerchiefs tied about their heads because they have the toothache.

Things began to go wrong again; there was more fighting, and Clinche's household went from bad to worse. It was in vain that his wife made concessions; the more she tried to smooth over difficulties the harder she found it to please her husband. Baptiste's thumb started to discharge when it had been thought cured; he complained of pains in his arm, and a lump began to form in his arm-pit. Constant Martin, the shop-keeper, failed. Lude had moved all his boundary stones and had thereby almost doubled the area of his ground, but he did not feel satisfied. He had the fever for gain. One is never too rich to imagine oneself richer still. And then after being land rich, there is money to acquire. Crowns and pieces of gold.

And so it was that on the 6th of January he went up to Essaims again, his top field—a large one, but the grass on it was thin, for it was too high. It seemed to him that he had been very generous to himself, because, by moving the boundary stones, he had absorbed at least a good third of the two neighbouring fields. Undoubtedly someone would notice it, but this did not disturb him; in fact for a second or two he felt it would be a good thing if it were discovered. He made a detour on account of the lately fallen snow, and all his footsteps remained in black, like letters that make words and phrases. But once he had taken this precaution, he made no further attempt at concealment. His personality was a comic mixture, almost like a barrel containing every sort of wine: pride, shame, false assurance, fear, heartiness, discouragement—a terrific mixture. He was wearing high gaiters, his eyes shone beneath a hat pulled down over his ears, and in spite of the biting cold, his long neck rose up from his woollen waistcoat without a scarf of any sort. On his way home he stretched it forward, plunging through the quickly forming drifts, sometimes almost up to his waist. What would he need to make him happy? Ten francs a day? No; make it fifteen; and it wouldn't do to have to earn them; they ought to come of their own accord at fixed times like rich people's dividends: money that is considerate, that presents itself to you, hat in hand. "Then I would feel myself a man," he thought.

He did not notice that night was approaching, but he was not far from the village. Suddenly everything changed colour. The greyness behind the evening clouds gave place to a mysterious green light that he could not explain on account of the fact that there were neither stars nor moon. The snow had become transparent in it and the hills and boulders were great black ill-defined masses. Further down, the roofs of the village rocked in his vision. They looked like an enormous pile of pebbles, and the church steeple like a stick emerging from it. Lude could see quite well enough to find his way, but everything seemed strange, and every now and then he drew his hand across his eyes. "Surely all this is in my head, all this rocking back and forth." He laughed and did not recognise the sound of it, but he soon got to his house.

A lamp was lit in the kitchen; his wife would be waiting for him, but somehow he could not bring himself to go in. He went up to the window, and flattening himself against the wall, he peered in. Little Marie was sitting at the end of the table with a book before her, and he could see her lips moving. It was undoubtedly one of her school books; she was studying her lesson, and he could see that she was carefully spelling out each word. When she had got to the end of a phrase she bent over with her eyes shut, said it to herself, and sat up straight again. The lamp hanging from the ceiling shed a pleasant light upon her round forehead and her drawn-back hair. Everything in there was perfectly calm. The fire burned on the hearth and the plates were on the table round the porridge bowl. Adele appeared at that moment with a faggot and broke some sticks across her knees. Jean Lude saw all this, but he could not bring himself to go in.

He jumped back as his wife entered the room, fearing that she would see him. Then he saw the green light again, but it was dimmer now because his eyes had become used to the bright light at the kitchen window. He could not stay there, but where should he go? He thought of the shed; there at least no one would see him. First of all he had to decide what to do; he had no plans for the night, so he walked around the house, and that gave him time to think. He came to the door of the shed, entered, and sat down on an old plough. His knees came up to the level of his face, and it was not long before his head fell forward and rested upon them. "May the good Lord deliver me even if I have to keep on in my evil ways to be delivered. When I'm in a tunnel the direction I move in doesn't matter so much as the getting out." He ground his teeth together, and desperate projects rose up in his mind: breaking into houses at night; taking off one's shoes; an old woman sleeping, hardly necessary to disturb the bed; who would imagine she had not died a natural death? In a cupboard nearby, beneath a pile of sheets, a wallet swelling with bank notes...! "Good, that's it." He felt better, lifted up his head, and took some deep breaths. Then he discovered that there was no old woman, no wallet. Only the darkness coming in through the half-open door. He let his head fall forward again.

Thus it was that he did not notice the sound of approaching steps. It was only the creaking of the door that caused him to look up. He saw a vaguely outlined figure squeeze in through the opening and he heard a voice:

"Ah, I thought I'd find you in here."

The figure seemed to draw closer to him, but it was so dark in the shed that it was only the sound of the voice which enabled Lude to discover who it was. Shivers ran down his back, but he said to himself it was only the cold, and anyhow he had nothing to fear from the person who had entered the shed. It was Criblet, whom they called Serpent on account of his long thin body and his deceit. He did not count for much because drink had carried him to the depths.

"What do you want?" asked Lude.

"Nothing," replied Serpent.

Then came a silence; perhaps Serpent was going away.

"What a funny idea to hunt for me in this shed," thought Lude. "No one saw me come in here! It's on the end of my tongue to ask—how shall I keep it back? Oh, well, so much the worse for me if I risk it."

"Tell me, Criblet."

"What?"

"How did you know I was here?"

"By having two eyes in my head," Criblet replied, then he laughed and went on. "I'm glad you asked that question, now I can go on. I like walking, and I've just been up to look, at the stones…"

"What! " interrupted Lude breathlessly.

The other man noticed nothing and went on:

"There are all kinds up there, big and little. Some are too heavy, but there are some that can be lifted… One can take them like this with one's hands and pull them…" "Shut up," shouted Lude. "So you see," rejoined Serpent, and he began to laugh softly, "it's like clock-work. No need to be frightened when one speaks the truth. Some stones are light enough to move. Now I can speak freely. How much money have you got in there?"

Lude did not try to protect himself; he did not even think of lying.

"I've got about a hundred francs."

"Go and get them."

The Bible says the last shall be first, and Lude walked unsteadily into the house. Adele wanted to say something, but he told her to keep still.

He went into the bedroom and she tried to follow him, but he pushed her from him. He came out again, she looked at him, and he told her not to follow. With the key that hung on a nail he locked the front door behind him. He walked back to the shed, his legs weak beneath him, and Criblet, moving about in the darkness, was coughing a little as though he were catching a cold. Lude took the money from his pocket and said to Criblet:

"It's a hundred francs."

"Good," muttered Criblet as he took them from Lude's hand in the darkness. Lude tried to see Criblet, but he heard only his voice. Then the long sinuous body was vaguely apparent at the doorway. It stopped and turned slightly.

"Thanks," and Lude heard another little cough, "when this is gone, I'll come back."

The footsteps died away, and Lude wondered whether it had been a dream: "No, not a dream! He's got me all right. He knows my secret, and he can do what he likes with me, because he knows what I've done." He collapsed on the floor of the shed as though his legs had been cut off, but stood upright almost at once. Anger gave him fresh strength and his blood began to boil. The anger caused by Criblet's injustice propelled him swiftly. He could not have got very far away yet. The only thing was to follow him. "I'll get him," he thought; no one was about, and in the green light Lude followed Criblet. From beneath his hat he would be able to see the exact spot to aim at; he would have to strike quickly like a cat. He had been right a while ago. He could not stay in that tunnel. He was getting on well now, and he knew that the more he indulged in evil methods the easier it became to forget what evil was. One made use of them without regret.

Lude was now very close to Criblet, strangely close, he thought, and Criblet did not seem to notice him at all. The blow was struck just in time, and the shock of it caused Criblet to fall forward on his face with Lude on top of him.

"I've got him, I've got him," he cried, but he had not really. How could it have happened?

45

It was Lude who was on his back now, and Criblet had his hands round his neck and his knee on his chest. They rolled over and over, and there was a big hole in the snow where they had fallen; Criblet smiled out of one corner of his mouth.

"You're done for now, my poor Lude."

Criblet shook himself like a dog coming out of water, and little pellets of snow dropped out of his ears; then: "I mean you can't get along that way any longer."

Then raising his voice, so that each word was echoed back to him in the stillness that hung over the village, he shouted: "And the rest of you come and see if you like. Come and see what happens when a man cares too much about living upon other people!"

And he would have continued his shouting, but Lude at that moment got to his feet, and before Criblet could catch him, made his escape.

◊◊◊

The next morning the sun shone; during the night the moon had been dispersing the clouds; they now vanished quickly, and the sun took possession of the blue sky, almost causing the pale round moon to disappear.

Joseph arose early, for he had work to do in the woods; Héloïse got up with him, though Joseph had said to her:

"In your condition you would have done better to stay in bed."

And she answered as though jealous:

"That would be the last straw."

She was an industrious little woman, and in spite of all he could say she lit the fire, filled the kettle, ground the coffee, and put out the cups. Joseph was packing his lunch into a knapsack, and soon they were sitting at table with the metal coffee pot between them, the little drops falling into the container beneath the filter.

The lamp was lit, and Joseph could see the blue veins in his wife's cheeks. He got up from the table:

"Listen, you must promise to go back to bed when I've gone."

She promised, and he went off with an easy mind. A group of men were waiting for him at the Cross, and they started up the road together.

She watched them from the window for a long time, then she remembered her promise to go back to bed. How could she do that when the sun was shining; who would do her work? And anyhow, she thought, Joseph wouldn't need to know. So she did not keep her promise. She felt full of energy and good spirits. She began to sing, and the baby kept her from feeling lonely. Sometimes he kicked and she straightened up frowning, but soon a smile spread over her face. What if he did turn and twist and hurt her; it was only a sign that he was there. The more she suffered for him the more she would love him. She looked at herself, wondering: "Poor little thing! I wonder if he has room enough. He can't breathe or see; he can't hear or eat. No wonder he takes it out on me!" She was filled with pity and great happiness at the same time. She had only to be patient for a while: "Kick me thirty times if you want to. I won't complain."

This was why she liked to be alone just now; the neighbours complained that she was getting proud. "But," as she said to herself, "I've got someone to keep me company now, and the time passes too quickly for me to waste it chatting with everybody as I used to do."

It was soon ten o'clock; she took off her apron, hung it on a nail, and made herself tidy. Then she set forth to do her marketing. She wrapped herself in a shawl and wound a woollen scarf—black with a brown border—about her head.

In the brilliant sunlight the snowy streets shone like the dented surface of a caldron, and all the fence rails carried fringes of tiny icicles. The roofs each had one silver slope and one blue.

A lot of people were collected about the fountain, and she was afraid someone would stop her, so she kept on her way taking careful little steps. But the women had seen her and came running up to tell her that Lude had gone away. This was the great piece of news that had gone the rounds of the village that morning. Think of it, Lude had disappeared! His wife could not find him, and, according to Criblet, he had done well to go: at night he had been moving his boundary stones. Criblet had seen him, and Lude had been afraid. Criblet had thought him possessed, and declared that he had smelled sulphur.

Héloïse kept aloof from it all. Her life was full of another thing just now, wasn't it? She had soon got clear of the women and was approaching the shop where Brouque, the grocer, was awaiting her; he had a long black beard, hardly ever spoke at all, and he weighed out her salt quickly, then the flour. That made two parcels, two pounds each, and they went into her basket. She gave him seventy centimes and walked out into the sunlight.

At the fountain they were still discussing the event of the night before, so she went back by another way in order not to have to stop again. It was quieter there; no one was about except the people who lived in the street. There were some hay-sheds, two or three houses, and then Branchu's shop at a sharp turning. The snow was thick and frozen hard, and Héloïse had to be careful. One of her friends, named Julie, saw her coming and the two stopped for a moment's chat.

"It's unbelievable, just the same," Julie said. "No one has ever known anything against him. A nice fellow, too! Happy and in love with his wife. What can he be thinking of to go away like that!"

"Yes, yes; I know…" said Héloïse, and they parted. But instead of going indoors, Julie stayed in the street, and later on she told the others: "I stayed to watch her because it was fun to see her walking like that, and I was cross with her for not talking to me. She is changed, I said to myself, and we knew each other when we were kids. I stood there wondering and I thought I would never have recognised her. A fine show there beneath her skirt; the flap of her apron wouldn't button. And it was freezing so hard; that was why she had to walk slowly with one hand held up to keep her balance. Some put stockings on outside their shoes. She walked on for about five minutes, and just in front of Branchu's shop—I remember perfectly—she turned to look in through the window. At that moment she stopped and straightened up just as if she was going to fall on her back, and then she gave a scream, one that still sounds in my ears. Then she bent forward holding her stomach with her hands. I started to run, and by the time I got to her she had fallen…"

They put her on a stretcher, covered her with a sheet, and she was carried, two in front and two behind, to her bed. Someone went at once for the mid-wife and the priest, but they came too late. And it was a fine boy after all. They looked and were astonished to find him so big and well formed. "What a pity," they said; "another month or two and he could have been saved." But could he really have been saved? He was already dead when he left his mother's womb.

Happily Héloïse knew nothing about it. The women bustling about, their high voices, their concoctions of herbs, the hot linen—she was conscious of none of these things. She was far away from them, far off in another world; she was laughing gaily now, and they said: "Much better that she does!" and in the same breath, "Isn't it sad? She was so happy over what was coming to her. She'd waited so long."

The talking and discussing was everywhere, indoors and outside in the street. Little groups were collected here and there, and one heard:

"Impossible!"

"I've got eyes, haven't I?"

"How did it happen?"

"We know nothing about it."

"But she was strong and well."

"Of course she was!"

"And she wasn't ill?"

"She'd never been so well before."

"Perhaps her basket was too heavy? Or maybe she was tired out with walking so carefully?"

They shook their heads. No, it wasn't that.

Tronchet, the baker, a little round man, came rolling out of his door like a white ball; the clock said noon and the big bell tolled. Etienne, son of Etienne and grandson of a third Etienne, was bellringer and the two other Etiennes had been bellringers too. When one is son of a bell-ringer and grandson of a bell-ringer, one has bells in one's stomach, and he understood his business. There was a woman cutting pickled beetroot in a salad bowl, and her hands were red; she shouted something from her window to a neighbour who shouted back at her. And a great uneasiness, came over them. Had not anyone noticed the ugly cloud that had risen up from the horizon quite two hours ago and still blotted out the sun?

For a long time people had been wondering—putting things together in their minds. The total was frightening: Musy hung, Baptiste's thumb, the children with croup, the women with epilepsy, the beasts that had died, the boys' fight, and Lude, and now Héloïse. Things didn't happen like that; it wasn't natural.

Meanwhile Joseph came down from the forest and asked to see *him* first. They hardly dared to, but gave in when he became angry. He kept his hat on, and the odour of moss and bark had come down from the mountain with him. Little puffs of cold air were caught in the folds of his clothes. Someone lifted the sheet that covered the baby, and Joseph's head fell forward.

After a moment of silence, he asked:

"Did the priest come in time?"

"No, he was too late."

"Then my boy's soul won't go up there."

In a hollow voice Joseph continued:

"Not even that...! Not even that...! Poor little chap! What harm could he have done to be punished like this? Or have we ourselves sinned in some way?"

There was no answer to his questionings, and they saw him sink down upon a chair, his body gradually crumpling like earth falling away from a bank in a thaw.

He remained motionless for a moment, and then suddenly asked:

"Where is she?"

They took him into the bedroom, and Héloïse began to laugh when she saw him at the door, but they had told him she had a high temperature.

No one could tell whether or not he had understood. She was not looking at him; her eyes were gazing into another world and the fever had blotched them with white. She was quite still now, and her arms lay at her sides as though they did not belong to her. She said nothing; she only laughed and laughed. What would he do? Would he burst into tears? Would he throw himself upon her to make her stop laughing? Would he take hold of her hand?—He did none of these things. He simply looked at her and said:

"It isn't Héloïse any longer; someone's changed her."

Then he turned away shaking his head slowly as though he had never been in the room before:

"Who is it that's changed her?"

There was anger in his voice now:

"Who is it that's changed her?"

He stamped his foot and shut his jaws tight. Someone took him by the shoulders:

"Joseph, be calm."

But he kept on asking angrily:

"Who's changed her? Who's changed her?"

He went into the kitchen with the rest and sank down upon a bench; his clothes seemed suddenly to be too large for him. His friends spoke to him, but he did not seem to hear; they questioned, but he did not answer. Big Communier came and put his hand on his shoulder.

"Look here, Joseph; you're not being a man. Perhaps your wife needs you."

Joseph raised two unseeing eyes and a closed mouth to him and simply shrugged his shoulders as if to say: "What can I do? There is nothing left of me either." And the change that suddenly came over him was the more noticeable on account of his first bewilderment. He straightened up and exclaimed:

"Listen, Communier! I would like to know how this happened."

Communier was glad:

"We'll tell you as much as you want to know." And he began to tell it all; how Héloïse had gone out at about ten o'clock to do some shopping, and how she had stopped to talk at the fountain. All that had been seen was related to him.

"She took a back street on her way home…"

At this point Joseph looked up quickly.

"She stopped again and spoke to Julie. Just after that it happened."

"Where was it?" Joseph asked.

"Just in front of the new shoemaker's shop."

Joseph stood up and said: "I knew it perfectly well." He was not at all like the Joseph of a few moments before; there had been a strained expression then, but now his features fell back into place, his complexion regained its colour, and his eyes shone:

"I thought so!" He raised a hand and continued speaking in a determined voice:

"We are punished for not having listened before. He saw the truth of it, and now he's dead."

"Who do you mean?"

"Luc, of course!"

They did not understand at first, but little by little they began to remember Luc's prophecies. Perhaps he had been right. Thus the idea took form and the six men with Joseph were soon of his mind: Communier, Meyru, Brandon, Tonnerre, and the two Jan brothers.

"We'll come with you," they declared, and Joseph said:

"We must keep our heads at first, but if he doesn't say

what we expect him to, if he should hesitate, ever so little…!"

He said no more but raised a clenched fist, and they felt he had taken a terrible resolution.

So these seven men set forth, and the women stayed with Héloïse. The men had not far to go—a hundred yards at the most. When they reached the sharp turning in the street the fine blue signboard confronted them.

Joseph, stepped up to the window of the shop and knocked on the pane. Branchu was there, and the others were afraid that Joseph might not be able to contain his anger, that he might insult him or even knock him down. But the expected did not happen. Branchu opened the window and asked Joseph what he could do for him; Joseph had no answer to make.

It was all because the shop was so quiet. Its occupant had been peacefully waxing his thread, and at the knock he had turned towards them the face of a man who was only thinking of his job. He had put down his hammer and placed his work upon a chair. Was that how a man with something on his conscience would behave?

"Please come in," said Branchu to Joseph, and seeing the others, "and your friends too, if they will give me that pleasure."

Perhaps he thought they wanted to order something— Joseph on his side was completely at a loss; he was speechless, and could only shake his head. In a moment or two they were all in the street again, and Branchu watched them go, leaning on the window sill. He too seemed not to have understood, and he looked as though he were saying to himself that undoubtedly there had been some mistake. A rosy light glowed everywhere as four o'clock struck; the big cloud was still blotting out the sum, for it moved in the sky at the sun's pace and covered it like an eye-lid. Some rays, however, struck down through the fringes of the cloud and fell upon the mist that hung over the village, just below the level of the bell-tower. Behind the village the steep ascent reared itself up in obscurity, and finally ended in a peak that overlooked the surrounding country. At the very top was a cross—a real Calvary. It was easy to imagine the soldiers climbing up to it by the little winding roads, then there would be the people impelled by curiosity, and then the holy women. But somehow He whom these had followed was not there, in spite of what Lhôte had declared.

Poor abandoned souls that they were! There was no Presence with them. Nothing but the undertone of anxiety everywhere in the village: a lamp shone in Joseph's house; Héloïse's fever went higher; and Joseph sat alone in the kitchen. Her laughing and the endless talk of the women in her room were too much for him. The fire went out because no one thought of keeping it up.

He held out a few moments longer and then came a tingling in his eyes. He breathed two deep breaths, and tears fell at last—a man's silent tears. He did not even think of trying to stop them, and they rolled down over his cheeks and fell one by one on to his trousers.

CHAPTER IV

◊

The President was a very prudent man and seldom allowed himself to be disturbed, but he was forced into taking steps now. Towards the middle of March one of the prettiest chalets of the parish was carried away by an avalanche, and a few days later the hamlet of Essertes was completely destroyed by fire.

The President began to perceive that people thought it strange of him to do nothing; what was there to do? But they came to him saying: "We can't go on like this any longer." And then: "It's your duty to think of something to do." So he finally decided upon a course of action, and after reflecting at great length, he went to see the only man he thought could help them—the priest.

The priest's house was close to the church; it was grey and three stories high, and had a granite porch, approached by two flights of steps, in the centre of the bare façade. Just as the President was mounting the steps, the thing which he was least expecting happened. The door opened and Branchu, of all people, appeared. It was difficult to believe but impossible not to, for it was he, and there was a large parcel under his arm.

The President stood stock still, but Branchu seemed in no way embarrassed. He looked in excellent spirits and smilingly doffed his hat to him. He might even have stopped to chat if the President had not turned his head away.

So Branchu went on, and the President mounted the steps. Alas, he had to! A wide arched stairway led to the second floor, and he climbed it slowly, trying, as he went, to collect his thoughts. But he did not succeed, and anyway there was not time. The priest made him sit down at once; otherwise he would have fallen. What could it have been? The heat, or the thick tobacco smoke? He thought he saw empty glasses and a bottle on the disordered table; then everything swam before his eyes.

A big, deep voice restored his equilibrium:

"Well, Mr. President, what brings me the pleasure of this visit?"

There were no longer any glasses or a bottle on the table; only the priest looking at him—a big man with a red face and neck. He had enormous shoulders, and the size of his stomach showed a weakness for food and wine rather than for prayers and saying Mass. He kept looking at the poor President with impatience, and had to repeat his question before any reply could be dragged out of him. Suddenly words came pouring forth:

"You must excuse me, Father; but we need you so badly, so badly. We don't understand what it is that is happening to us. Misfortunes, of course, but they never cease! Still, it isn't so much that. It's something I hardly know how to explain—like a power being exercised over us. It's like a fever that makes the good people among us bad, and the bad worse. And now the Chalet des Entraigues has been carried away, and Essertes entirely wiped out by fire; men, women, and children are dying; every kind of sickness is breaking out. And we fear the future, for things are getting worse. We don't know what to do... It isn't natural! We wondered, Father, whether you wouldn't come to our assistance because..." He could say no more.

"All this doesn't surprise me!" said the priest. Then he struck the table with his fist. He was no longer red but purple.

"These deaths, all this mourning, these diseases, the

beasts dying; don't you deserve it? Well, I should say so, and you may well pity yourselves." He struck the table again. "Have I not warned you? Liars and fornicators that you are! The strange thing is that your punishment is not more terrible. God is more patient than I am. And when misfortunes come to you, you don't seem to understand why." He took a quick breath and then held his nose: "I tell you that you smell horribly; you smell of corpses. Listen, there is only one way out, and that is to change your habits. Let the liars lie no more and let the blasphemers cease their blasphemy. You see it's a simple method." He burst out laughing, and then: "You might as well expect a river to flow towards its source, or snow in the summer time. Why, confound…" He stopped abruptly, remembering perhaps a little late that he owed a certain reverence to the garments he wore. He calmed himself and mopped his forehead, seeming now to be greatly embarrassed. The President had not moved from his chair. A moment of silence followed, and then the priest arose. From the corner of the room he took up his gun: "Look at this, Mr. President, isn't it a fine weapon…? Ah, I forgot, you are not a sportsman."

The President got up too, and shook his head.

"A hammerless," continued the priest, "worth at least five hundred francs. I got it for a song. Just look at it!" He turned it over and worked the spring. "It's as carefully made as a clock, and I can't say that of my parishioners."

He laughed again, a mocking laugh, and the President looked at him, without understanding what he said, and weighed down by the reproaches that he personally did not deserve. He had had a good impulse, and this was how it had been repaid. "Another time," he said to himself, "I won't bother to come."

Just as he arrived at his own door, the biggest bell in the Church Tower sent forth a muffled peal; its bronze rim was struck by the end of the clapper and the sound seemed to come up out of the earth itself. It was like a deep moan. Then another, and another; and the people in the streets, in the woods, digging potatoes, cutting back the hedges, the goatherd watching his goats, and the old woman making a fire of dead-wood—all asked the same question:

"Who is it now?" And they crossed themselves.

Boom! There is grief in men's hearts. Wherever they are, whatever they do, they are always looking into the face of Death. A moment of forgetfulness and She comes before them.

Boom! My grandfather and my grandmother are dead, my Aunt Fridoline is dead, my little brother Jean is dead, my little brother Pierre is dead, my sister Martine is dying, and I shall die too.

Boom! Father in Heaven, help us in our affliction; without You we are nothing; we need You terribly; Father in Heaven, pity us in our sorrow.

Boom! I didn't know anyone was so ill. I didn't see the Holy Sacrament go by. Maybe it's for old Borchat. He had to have blood drawn.

Boom! The day was cold and grey. A hundred men and a hundred women were black against the snow. The men walked ahead of the women, and the bier was covered by a black cloth with ornaments of silver that represented a death's head and two crossed bones. The pall bearers kept step so as not to shake the body. The procession passed the fountain. Little beards of ice hung from the eaves of the houses; the big lime-tree was leafless, and looked as though it were made of wire. There was no sound save that of iron-spudded shoes striking the frozen street, and the deep crushing note of the big bell. They went into the church; up to the screen supported by the low wall. There were wooden crosses, painted blue, from which hung pearl crowns and beneath each of these was a bell-glass covering a bouquet with an inscription and two joined hands. The procession advanced towards the altar; Joseph was in the first group and he had already to be supported. At the grave there were two men, each holding him by an arm. Had he been to the church? He did not know; he knew nothing now; he felt nothing. Between the two men he swayed like a tree sawn nearly through at its base, sideways, forward and backward, but he went through it all—he had to go through everything! He saw his past, his hopes, his very reason for existence descending into the earth: "My God, it isn't possible! My backbone has gone; she was my heart of hearts, the centre of my thoughts." He groaned and wrung his hands, and they told him to try to be calm, but he kept on groaning as though someone had plunged a knife into his stomach to turn and twist it. Poor Joseph Amphion! He had been promised a baby, but now it was dead and his wife too. Then he began to think: "Wasn't I always good to her; didn't I act towards her as I promised to act the day I put the ring on her finger? And when she was writhing on her bed and I was saying unjustly, 'She is no longer herself,' if I had gone to her and kissed her might she have been saved by love? Might she have recognised me and said, 'You are there, Joseph'? Oh, she was better than me, my beautiful Héloïse, and now she's gone. It's my fault, all my fault!"

The earth fell upon the coffin, and he was led away. The rest of the procession followed and went into their houses hardly less miserable than Joseph. They were speechless because there was nothing to say. Silence hung over the village, and the big bell had stopped ringing. The dull sky descended till it almost touched the roofs; it seemed to enter the houses and remind the people of the desolation that enveloped them. They came out again like animals from their holes, and stood with bowed heads in little groups in the street.

◊◊

Other tragedies followed quickly. In less than two weeks three women on three successive days suffered the same misfortune as Héloïse. Branchu was there on all three occasions. Then came Herminie's turn.

About ten men were standing at the turning of the street. They saw Herminie coming towards them, and at that moment Branchu emerged from his shop. He turned to look at Herminie with his hands in his pockets and a strange smile upon his face. It was said afterwards that his eyes changed colour, but the one certain thing was that Herminie's attack of pain came at the very moment when Branchu's eyes were upon her. She too cried out; she too raised her arms; and she fell down as though her legs had melted under her. Branchu began to laugh (so it was said) and he spoke at the top of his voice (so it was said) :

"That makes five, not bad...?" The astonishing thing was that the men never thought of going for him. It was all over so quickly! During their bewilderment, Branchu had time to escape.

Excitement spread through the village; the first thing was to carry Herminie to her bed, and four of the men attended to this. The others ran through the streets stopping at each door to knock or push it wide open and shout, "Are you coming?" to which the reply was—"What's the matter?" But they passed on quickly to the other houses. The gathering occurred in front of the church, and weapons had been snatched up: forks, sticks, guns, scythes. Late arrivals asked, "What's it all about?" and the news had to be told over again. Arms were lifted up, heads were shaken, and several bursts of hysterical laughter rose above the excited voices.

"Why did we let it go on? How was it that we didn't guess sooner? Poor souls! A little longer and they would all have gone like that."

In spite of the unheard-of things that had happened, no one tried to discover by what means Branchu had been able to bring them about. Don't let's bother about that now, they decided; we know what he has *done*. That was what had brought them all together. To deal with such a man, the more people the better. The open space before the church soon became too small, and all they needed now was someone to lead them. Communier was the tallest, and every one shouted: "Are we ready? Come on, say the word, you're in command!"

Communier, though taken unawares, raised his arm to silence them for a moment:

"We'll go first to make sure he's not at his shop."

Then off they started; some by the street and others behind the houses. There were not only men in the prime of life, but the old and crippled too; women and children poured out into the street, or shouted from the windows and doorways. Some of the girls laughed because they were at the age when one laughs at everything, and under their lifted skirts, bright-coloured woollen stockings were visible.

Communier knocked at the door:

"Is anyone there?" Then he grasped his gun by the barrel and struck the door with the butt-end. One or two others joined him and it soon fell back. In they rushed, but no Branchu! It made no difference; they entered the house anyway. The window panes flew into bits. The beautiful blue signboard hung by one end, then it fell to the pavement and split in two. Meanwhile the roof was being dealt with from within by means of long poles, and heavy flat slates came tumbling down, leaving the rafters bare.

From the window of a house nearby came a tiny quavering voice: "What the devil are you doing?"

It was the old landlord, and nobody paid any attention. He could have piped his complaint all night long. Never was work so quickly or so neatly done; and when it was finished, they were breathless and pouring with sweat.

This accomplishment delighted them. They had been made fools of, and the desire to assert themselves was satisfied; not however until they had gone into the house again as though to re-destroy the destruction they had wrought, and had kicked about among the rubbish. After this their energy flagged, for there was nothing more to do and they were very tired.

Someone suggested searching the forest above the village, where the man was now believed to be hiding, but their number had diminished and their spirits were ebbing.

They started to climb the slope back of the village in order to discover tracks, but there were none visible upon the smooth white surface. In the road they were too numerous and too confused to pick out those of a single person; several chance clues were followed along different roads, and finally the whole party reached the forest. There was much careful searching, but without trace of anyone having entered it. Every now and then large grey-feathered birds rose up, frightened, to the security of the tangled branches above. They started a hare, but failed to catch it. Nothing else, nothing! And the further they climbed, the more thickly they found the wood populated by the tall white ghosts of tree trunks and boulders. It was difficult to make any progress, and the afternoon drew to a close, leaving the men discouraged and weary. The first wood was finally crossed; they came out on to a bit of level open ground and counted their number. The fact was soon evident that to cross the next wood would be too great an effort. It was much steeper than the first and ran all the way up to the ridge.

The men stood about for a few moments and then someone said: "If we're to get back before dark, we'd better be starting."

◇◇◇

They were ashamed to return without having accomplished anything, but there was hot coffee awaiting them, and big fires blazed in the kitchens. When they sat down to get warm, steam, rose up from their clothes:

"We did what we could. One thing's certain; there's an Evil Spell working against us."

There was a lot of whispering from ear to ear; indeed there were some things that could not be spoken aloud, and in this way every one heard the rumour that Lhôte had not been seen since Branchu's disappearance. Later, this was verified: Lhôte had been away all day, and old Marguerite awaited him anxiously. She was greatly troubled by all that had happened, for this man had saved her life. She had been at death's door, and he had come to her. Simply by taking her hand he had led her back to life. Was it not a debt? She could give all she possessed and still be under an obligation to this man who was being called wicked by everyone. They had destroyed his shop and had gone into the woods after him.

She was alone in the house, listening to the noises that still came to her from the village. Though it was late no one seemed to want to go to bed. It was like another Christmas night. The clock in the tower struck midnight, and she kept hearing people passing and re-passing her door; she could hear talking in the neighbouring houses, and every time she heard a footstep or a voice, she said to herself: "This time it's him."

But he did not come, and still she sat there by the fire in her old flat black bodice and full skirt. Little by little silence fell upon the village; one o'clock had struck and it was getting on toward two. She went into her bedroom and started to undress. At that moment she thought she heard someone groping to find the key-hole. Yes, there was someone trying to open the door. It was an old complicated lock with a secret latch; at last she heard the accustomed click. Without further hesitation she ran half-dressed into the kitchen and saw the door open slowly and noiselessly. Her son came in and put his finger to his lips. He then closed the door as carefully as he had opened it and came towards her.

"Mother," he said, whispering rapidly, "get me some bread, cheese, dried meat, and a bottle of wine. And I'll want some covers too, warm ones. The ones from my bed will do."

His last words caused her to ask: "And you...?"

He went on without answering:

"Please, Mother, hurry. It's late, and the darkness won't last much longer."

She stood motionless, so he went to the shelf and took down some food that he found there.

"Andre!" He turned to her. "Andre, you are my son; tell me everything..."

"What is there to tell?"

"Tell me what..."

"Don't you really understand, Mother?"

He straightened up and in the candle light she saw that his fine black eyes were shining. She looked at her big handsome son standing there in his soaking clothes. Then she went up to him and put her arms about his neck:

"Andre, don't forget that we have always lived together; it's cold out there and you'll catch your death. Stay with me! No one will know about it... *He* won't know it ...and they say he's a wicked man, too..."

He pushed her away and spoke aloud:

"Mother, you're the one that's forgetting. You were lying on this table and they said, 'She's lost!' That's not long ago, Mother. I haven't forgotten it!"

Her arms fell to her sides; there was nothing she could say.

"Let's do it quickly!" he said, but the old woman could hardly stand on her feet. He got a large basket and put the necessary provisions in it: bread, meat, and cheese. Then he folded up the covers from his bed and laid them on top. And his mother fidgeted about him, but her hands would not obey her, and she only succeeded in hindering his preparations. He had to do without her help. Just as he was going out he said:

"I'll come back tomorrow night; try and have everything ready for me." He had gone some minutes before she realised he had not kissed her.

The next night he came again and the three nights following; on the fourth it was freezing harder than ever and he was coughing violently when he came in. She felt she could endure it no longer, and when he had gone she said to herself:

"It's all that man; perhaps he'll die on account of him. It's true that he cured me, but if this is to go on I'd rather be dead." A heart could not be cut in two; the old woman understood this and she knew where her son's was. So on that fourth night in the moonlight she followed him secretly and discovered where the hiding-place was. She came down into the village again, and went to find Communier.

"I'll tell you this," she said, "but you must promise not to harm my son if he is with him. He's not bad himself, only this man has fooled him."

Communier replied that the bargain would be kept.

◊◊◊◊

The next morning they started before daylight; two groups had been formed in order to surround the place where the man was hiding. According to old Marguerite this place was beneath a thick hedge that ran along the top boundary of a field called *Les Moilles*; just above it there was a rocky slope falling all but perpendicularly into the valley beyond.

A thick fog almost prevented the second row of men from seeing the first, and it was as though the former were casting their shadows before them. Their only thought was to reach the spot undiscovered, and the fog, though confusing, was much better for their purpose than sunlight. They were careful to move noiselessly, and the snow made this fairly easy. It was like walking on cotton-wool or thick feathers. Silently they advanced, as though after partridges—the red-legged sort, that must be taken unawares. They were armed with poles, forks, and fork-handles, and to those with guns Communier had said: "If he tries to get away, fire on him."

Now they were climbing up the steep field; there were bare patches every now and then, where the snow had been blown away or had slipped down the slope, and they had to walk with great care upon the frozen ground. All this was easy for mountaineers, and it was not the first time they had climbed the slopes in winter. After all there was always wood to bring down, and also a good many of them were hunters. Finally they came close beneath the place where they had been told the man was hiding: the field called *Les Moilles*. The fog was still thick, and the slope was so steep that they had to use both hands and legs to climb it.

At that moment the wind began to blow, making caverns in the fog. These grew larger and larger, until at last the soft white ceiling started to break up. What had seemed a moment before to be a solid mass now looked like a lot of big white boulders sailing about and bumping each other gently. And then all of them rolled away down the sky.

Nothing could have been worse for the search party. The men flattened themselves out on the ground and crawled along for some minutes like that. Then, suddenly, a broad patch of sunlight fell upon them, and by craning their necks they could see the whole extent of *Les Moilles* and the woods beyond. The remains of the fog—little cushions of it—rested here and there, caught among the branches of the trees, but what interested them most was the high thorny hedge running across the top of the field, just beneath a high bank. The snow upon the hedge weighed down the upper branches of it, and formed a kind of roof beneath which were many deep recesses. In front of one of these the snow was beaten down and trampled.

The significance of this was perceived at once, and they began to run towards it, spreading out into a semi-circle. Just at this moment the other group appeared at the edge of the wood. No movement under the hedge! They drew near, and in the recess, roofed by thickly woven branches, Branchu slept.

The opportunity was too easy to be made use of, so they said: "We'll settle him later. At present we can be satisfied with stopping him from defending himself." And three of the more daring among them went for him. One got him by the neck, another by the arms, and another by the legs. A scuffle ensued, and Branchu was soon dragged out of his nook, and securely tied up.

He seemed neither to have thought of escaping nor even of defending himself; he did not even struggle, and he lay now on his back with his arms tied to his waist and a smile upon his face.

The men were no longer anxious, not caring whether he was smiling or not, now that they had him. Their spirits revived quickly, and pressing closely in around him, they shouted their jibes in his face. "We'll form a procession. Communier, you're not in command any more. He is the leader now."

They formed a column, two by two, and a place was arranged half way along for Branchu. It was the proper one for him, because, they said, "We who go before can tell who it is that is coming, and those who follow are the King's escort."

"King of Misfortune, we've got you in our power now." Two men lifted him up, and amid shouts of laughter they placed him on their shoulders.

"A King should sit like that—on a throne."

The procession moved forward by an unbeaten road, but it was easy for so many men to clear a way. Sticks and guns were shouldered, and a steady roar of laughter and shouting rose up from the marching column. Jokes passed back and forth, and the white expanse of snow gleamed and melted in the full sunlight.

"Even the sun is with us, on this festive day, as we escort our King. We carry him; it is the right of Kings to be carried; they always sit on thrones; and let us weave him a crown, and give him the rod of leadership to hold." They talked and scoffed, but did not slacken their pace, so that the village soon came into sight, rolled up tightly in its niche like a cat trying to keep warm.

Almost immediately the procession was seen, and people began to run up to meet it. An old woman was the first to join them, in spite of the fact that she was all bent over and stiffened with age. In the middle of the road she stopped and asked:

"Is he with you?"

The procession kept moving and so great was the noise of shouting and laughter that her question was not heard. They saw that it was old Marguerite, and guessed what she had come for, so someone shouted to her:

"No, we didn't see him."

They passed on quickly; she raised her arms and shook her head:

"What was the use? I've betrayed the man who saved me, and they didn't find my son. Ah, God, they've got the man who saved me!"

She saw they were carrying him and stretched out her hands, crying: "What's he done to you? What's he done to you?" She pushed in and tried to pull him down from their shoulders; but they threw her aside, and her cries were lost in the tumult of voices: "We're bringing our King. Honour him; he deserves it."

A woman stepped out of the crowd and spat in his face, then another, then a third. His carriers lowered him a little so that he was within reach, and more women did the same thing.

Joseph appeared at the door of his house as they passed it. He came out and struck the man's face with a branch of thorn until the blood flowed freely.

The procession moved on down the winding street past the fountain, and came to a halt in the crowded square. The column was replaced by a surging mass of people, and above the heads the man's body was borne along in the current, his face defiled, his eyes bleeding.

"What are you going to do with him?" cried the people.

"Cut off his head," came the reply.

"What are you going to do before that?"

"Tear out his finger-nails and his toe-nails; dig out his eyes; cut out his tongue; stick a red hot poker into his ears."

"And then what?" shouted someone.

"We'll nail him by the hands and feet to the barn door like a screech owl."

"That's the thing—nail him up."

A crowd of girls was standing on the bench that circled the big lime tree, and the ledges in front of the church windows were packed with little boys. The girls held their heads with both hands, and the boys craned their necks to see better what was going on. A huge circle was formed, and Branchu, in the I middle of it, turned and twisted, leaned forward, then straightened up, and sank from view. At that moment, two men pushed their way through to the centre. One carried a long pointed stick, and the other a blacksmith's hammer. The space in the middle grew larger; people drew back and then closed in around Branchu who was still invisible to all except those in front. The man carrying the stick raised it. Someone shouted:

"You're going to do it?"

"Of course," was the reply. Then the stick came down, again and again.

"They're going to kill him first!"

"No, no! Nail him to the door alive!" Others joined in:

"Yes, yes, nail him up alive!"

"Like a screech-owl."

"Like a filthy night-bird."

The man with the hammer started to laugh. His mouth was wide open but his laughter was inaudible. The man with the stick should have finished his work, for he had had help from those near him, but he kept on and called for more help. It was impossible to see, but Branchu was evidently being dragged along the ground towards a blue door in the church wall. The man with the hammer jumped on to the shoulders of some men near him, and a grey object was lifted up and placed against the blue door. Another man holding a knife mounted the crowding shoulders; then a sudden silence followed, during which Branchu's arms were freed from his body. His head was hanging over his breast; they stretched out his arms and the hammer was raised to drive in the nails...

Suddenly his laugh rang out, but no one waited long enough to notice that he had raised his head; his captors abandoned him and the men with hammer and knife jumped to the ground. To fly from the place was all they could think of; the square emptied; the streets emptied, and the noise of shutting doors could be heard throughout the village; then nothing but the sound of his laughing; and then—absolute silence. Silence and emptiness, save for the Man standing upright in the middle of the square in the sunlight. The ropes had fallen from his body, and upon his face there was no trace of blood or filth. His complexion was as fresh as though he had just risen from his bed, and his eyes shone brightly. No derangement of his clothes, not a spot or a tear anywhere, and he laughed again as he looked about him.

He took out his pipe, filled it, and was just lighting it when someone came running up to him:

"I've seen it all, and here I am." Lhôte fell on his knees before him, and continued:

"They spat on your face and tore your flesh with thorns."

Lhôte's voice sank lower and lower:

"They wanted to crucify you, but your power was revealed to them, for it is written—'He will reveal His power'..."

The Man looked at Lhôte silently; every now and then a puff of blue smoke issued from his mouth.

Then the old woman who had been watching for her son came towards them.

"Do what you like with me," she cried. "I think as you do and I love the One you love."

She was on her knees, but Lhôte drew himself up:

"Go away. I don't know you anymore."

The old woman fell forward with her face in the snow, and the others heard a chuckling behind them, someone spat and coughed gently. The third and last arrival was Criblet. He zigzagged across the square to join them. He never walked straight.

"I don't care whether you're Jesus or the Devil, but I know I'll be better off with you." He would have raised his arm, but did not dare to for fear of falling. He coughed again and wiped his mouth:

"I've already made a hundred francs, thanks to you. So—so I thought perhaps you'd see that I made the same amount again some time."

CHAPTER V

◊

A short time before this, Adele (whose husband, Lude, had gone away) called her little girl into the kitchen one morning, and asked her:

"Do you love me?"

"Oh, yes!" Marie assured her.

Adele wanted to, go on talking, but she had to stop. She stared vacantly before her. She looked like an old woman, though in reality only thirty-four, and what she had to tell Marie was a difficult thing to say to a little girl. It made her very unhappy, but after a few moments' silence she made a fresh start:

"If you love me then, Marie, will you come away with me?"

"Yes, mother," she replied.

"But I haven't told you where we're going yet. We'll be all alone and you'll have to stop going to school. You won't have any more friends to play with."

"But you're a nicer friend than all the others." Marie was a neatly dressed little girl with pretty eyes and tightly drawn-back hair. Her forehead shone and her face was rather pale.

Adele took her on her knees. What a sweet consolation she was after all! All was quiet except for a cracking noise every now and then, as though someone were walking on the roof; the frozen cap of snow was beginning to melt.

"Don't you see, darling, we can't stay here. I thought of the little house up in the mountains. Up there we'll be away from everything, all alone. But I never feel lonely with you, dear."

"I don't feel lonely with you either," Marie replied.

Adele kissed her, and it was with difficulty that she drew her lips away from the little girl's mouth. The cracking sound on the roof was heard again; lumps of snow began to fall from the eaves.

Suddenly Marie asked: "Will father come too?"

"Oh, yes, he'll come."

"When will he come?"

"Not yet," said Adele, "because he's gone on a long journey, but of course he'll come back." She lowered her head to hide the tears that trembled at her eyelids. She had to be brave and cheerful; that was her duty and it was the hardest of all. Since the departure of her husband she had had to take all the punishment for his wrong doing, and bear with the ill will of her neighbours. They were always asking:

"Have you heard anything from that robber husband of yours?"

Many people had begun to cut her, and others talked to her with a sham sympathy that made her suffer more than if they had refused to notice her at all. It had not taken her long to understand that she would have to give in.

But there can be no real loneliness when one has given one's heart. A gap is soon bridged over by love; it gradually rebuilds shattered foundations and fills in empty spaces. Adele had accepted the situation and a new courage came to her. The preparations for their departure were soon completed, and at dawn the mule stood waiting at the door. One grey linen bag held their provisions, another their clothes; and the big iron saucepan, with its feet upwards was tied to the saddle.

They locked the door, and there were tears in Adele's eyes: "Take a good look, Marie. Heaven knows when we'll see our house again."

"Don't cry, darling," Marie said as she took charge of the goat. Adele wiped her eyes and grasped the mule's bridle.

A good half of the village had to be crossed, but they met no one, though it was the time when people were usually in the streets for a breath of air and gossip. The village was soon left behind, and the road began to rise up steeply, winding its way past the fields to the woods above. Every now and then they saw big grey birds with red heads start up from the snow-powdered hedges.

◊◊

The Man installed himself at the Inn. Simon with his wife and children had abandoned it hastily when they saw him coming.

The Inn had four bedrooms in it as well as a wine room, a big kitchen, and a full cellar—and Criblet was there, for it now cost him little to drink, eat, and sleep. There were two or three cases of macaroni, a big bag of rice, a cask of herrings, and plenty of sausages and hams were hanging in the fireplace. He made a visit to the cellar and tapped all the kegs one after the other, and when he emerged he wore a look of great satisfaction.

The Man and Lhôte and Criblet got on well together, and everything was peaceful. The Man seemed to be quite happy; Lhôte did not talk much and kept to himself a good deal. Criblet descended into the cellar with his jug empty and came up with it full to sit quietly .by the window. Ten or twelve glasses caused nothing extraordinary, but the thirteenth acted like a penny pushed into a musical-box, and a song twenty-five couplets long would commence to pour out of him, accompanied by a silly wagging of his head. Hours would pass like this—no movement except his wagging head and his hand performing the pleasant task of raising the glass to his lips. It was an easy life, but the arrival of Clinche was upsetting.

Clinche was the first of the village people to come to the Inn. He arrived one day towards evening, and they told him to come in and have a drink.

"My wife is making my life impossible. I've tried to get her to stop it, but nothing is any good. I've done with her, and I said I was going to clear out." He drew in a long breath and seemed to enjoy it.

"It's much nicer here with you; if these gentlemen wouldn't mind…"

The Man simply said: "There's room."

So Clinche became the fourth, and did not regret it.

They felt that from now on the Man would be able to do as he liked. The village streets were always empty; none of the villagers dared to emerge without being sure that the Man was not in sight. To see him was a signal to run for dear life and close the door behind. Fortunately he hardly ever left the Inn, so that it was generally possible for them to slink out to their stables or to go for water at the fountain, but nothing more than this could be attempted. They always returned from these short errands running, and stayed behind closed doors, for, as they said, "He might come and plant Himself on us as he did on Simon."

An astonishing sort of underground existence imposed itself upon the village. There had never been anything like it. Even the smoke from the chimneys seemed heavier than usual, and it clung to the roofs as though afraid to rise up and drift away on the wind. Life slackened pace in every way, and horrible diseases began to break out, one of which attacked the beasts. The cows got softening of the udder; and when they were milked, their teats tore off in one's hands. There was plenty of milk, but they suffered terribly, for it was impossible to take it from them. Day and night they could be heard mooing to each other from stable to stable.

The most surprising thing was that some people's cows escaped the disease; there was a kind of inverted justice about it. The more exemplary the lives of the owners, the worse they were punished; and those who gave themselves up to evil passions, covetousness, greed, laziness, and drunkenness suffered no loss. Some stables were empty, and in others not a single cow was touched by the disease. It was like the Bible story of the Angel who marked certain doors with blood and passed the others by.

Old Marguerite had lost her two goats; there was nothing to eat in her cupboard. Again she went to her son at the Inn, and again he said:

"Go away, I don't know you any longer."

And it was the same with the village people when she appealed to them:

"Why didn't you come to us first?"

She went back to sit before her dying fire; she knew the end was near, so she took her old shawl and wrapped it about her head. It was snowing, and she walked until she reached the quarry where the road came to an end. There she hesitated and seemed to be trying to decide whether to go on or to return to the village—a tiny, wizened, disconsolate figure. The big snowflakes whirled around her.

Finally she made up her mind. Why not make one more attempt? She went back into the village; night had come now, and she heard singing at the Inn. The shutters were closed so she went to the door and struck it with both hands, calling out to him. No reply came and she called again; still no answer. They had no need of her there. She met one or two hurrying figures in the streets, but when she tried to stop them they only quickened their pace.. No one needed her, no one in the whole village, and she listened to the sound of the last door being bolted.

She thought of her dead fire and her empty cupboard, and this time there was no hesitation in her mind, so she set forth again, left the village, passed the quarry, and entered the pine forest. She walked resolutely through the snow, saying to herself, "I'll keep going as long as I can, and when I have to stop, then I can do it." It was quite dark, and she kept bumping into the tree trunks; many times she slipped on the frozen ground and barely escaped falling. "What difference does it make whether I fall or not, whether I go straight or not, or slowly or quickly? All roads lead where I want to go, and one is as good as another."

A great indifference came to her, but one question still remained unanswered:

"Why did he cure me if this was to happen? My God, why did he cure me?" And she walked on and on in the darkness.

The way became steeper, the snow piled higher, and the night got darker and colder; soon her legs refused to obey her, and her head felt thick and numb. It seemed to her that she had got out of the forest now, but she was not quite sure. One step sideways, one backwards, and then she saw that the ground rose slightly on her right, "Why not here?" she said, and all she had to do was to let herself fall sideways towards the bank into something very soft. She drew up her knees, like a little baby in its cradle; then she clasped her hands around them, and her head fell forward.

And it snowed faster and faster.

◊◊◊

The people themselves now began to suffer from a skin disease; they scratched themselves until the blood came. Then black ulcers appeared on their faces, and these spread little by little over their foreheads, cheeks, mouths, and chins, until the victims looked as though they were wearing masks for a carnival.

For the most part the disease attacked tall people; the children were taken in a different way. Their arms and legs were all twisted up by it. The healthiest and best fed among them went into convulsions and came out of them in a pitiful state: their little backs bent, their legs in semi-circles, and the palms of their hands turned outwards.

They cried and cried, and the sound of their crying mingled with the mooing from the stables and the groaning and grumbling of their parents. People fled from each other, hating to look upon what they were themselves, or fearing further contagion.

They understood that life would soon be impossible. All the neighbouring villages had been asked for assistance, but the news of their misfortunes had gone everywhere; no one would come to help, and they soon saw that assistance would have to come to them from above. A meeting was arranged to talk about it. They hardly dared to look at each other; several had their heads wrapped in linen, and some concealed their hands in their sleeves, for the disease had not confined itself to people's heads.

It was decided that another visit should be paid to the priest, though no one had seen him for a long time and he seemed not to care in the least what happened to the village. They waited until evening, and then five or six of them, amongst whom were Communier and a pious little man named Jean-Pierre, the oldest inhabitant of the village, went to the priest's house by a back street so as to avoid passing the Inn. They knocked for some time without success, but finally a noise of furniture being pushed about was heard; then an inside door opened and shut, and he stood before them.

"There are more of you this time," said the priest. Then he burst out laughing and continued:

"Oh, I know why you've come, but you're too late. Punishment must take its course; no one can interfere with that."

He laughed again and the delegation entered. It was too dark in the room to see anything clearly, and they felt a strange uneasiness. Several moments of silence followed, after which Communier spoke:

"We're in such a terrible state. Father, that you must help us to..."

Someone interrupted: "This man keeps on..."

"What man?" asked the priest in a troubled voice.

A third voice joined in—a tiny voice like a child's, except that it trembled slightly. It was old Jean Pierre:

"Ah, Father, that's just the trouble. Nobody knows who he is. If we only knew, it would be different. We haven't lost our faith, Father, and that's why we're here now. We thought, maybe, that if we offered a prayer to God, He would hear it—a prayer from us all, I mean, for He never listens to one voice."

There was a general shaking of heads. They waited, but the priest made no answer. He strode up and down the room, and all they could see was his tall black figure moving swiftly in the obscurity. Then suddenly he spoke again:

"The first thing is to mend your ways!" He spoke at the

top of his lungs; he almost shouted. "That will find more favour with God! Don't you understand? To sin against Him and then proceed to the Church, with banners flying—that's far too easy. You must repent first, I tell you!"

Uneasiness grew upon them. Was it because of the brutality in his voice and his strange tone of insincerity? Perhaps he was right, after all. But then he was their only chance of salvation. So they stuck to their guns. No one moved; and when Jean-Pierre began his entreaties again, they all joined in, mumbling indistinctly:

"Please, Father, please."

The priest sat down at the table, and so far as they could tell, he was holding his head in his hands. Then he spoke to them in a low trembling voice:

"You are right. It is my business to help you, and I must do so."

Just what happened then no one knew exactly, except that everybody had stood up, and the priest too. When they hurried away, the thing had been arranged for the following Sunday.

Days of suffering followed, days that seemed three times their usual length, and Sunday seemed as though it would never come. Every minute brought fresh agonies, and the worst of it was that Time could not be managed like one's beasts when they stopped to drink or to crop grass. Alas, it was not possible to beat Time with a stick.

However, the prospect of the procession seemed to give the people courage. "Perhaps," they said. "Who knows?"

Everyone who was physically able joined it, and the church was three-quarters full. People had come singly, or in little groups, threading the dark alleys with hands stretched forward into the obscurity. Above; the roofs could be seen the church steeple surmounted by the cross, a vague shadowy cross against the sky, but a clear enough guide to follow. Every now and then the rough breathing of a beast, or the wail of a suffering child, or the sighing of someone in the agony of death could be heard behind a door. Never was there a moment of the day or night when the people's afflictions could be forgotten.

The gathering in the church was quickly accomplished, and a faint grey light began to filter through the little panes of the lofty windows. First came Mass, with the organ, voices, and chimes, and there was a visible security there within the walls of the Church. But another and a more effectual security that could not be seen reassured the people's hearts, so that, when the last words were said and the last response given, they left the church with a firm conviction that their troubles would soon be over.

It had been arranged that all the bells should be rung, and Etienne, son of Etienne, son of a third Etienne, went up into the tower. But he was not alone, for on that day there was more work than I usual. Big Marie-Madeleine was to be rung, and she required three men to manage her. First of all a tiny clear voice with vivid silvery notes came down to them from the heavens, like the song of a sky-lark. A man in a surplice carried the cross out of the church; he was one of the white-robed ones, and the women and the girls of the white robe would follow him. The cross had to be tilted forward for a moment because of the low portal, but it was soon upright again, and at that moment the little silvery note in the sky burst like a pod of ripe seeds: a thousand new notes poured forth and streamed downwards until they seemed to come out of the very air itself, above and beneath, rising and falling, approaching and receding.

The cross turned at the corner of the cemetery, followed by the white-robed men and the white robed women, and four young girls carrying a beautiful wax Virgin in silk robes. Then, as the people themselves began to come out of the Church, Big Marie-Madeleine's voice was heard. All the little chimes seemed to have fled helter-skelter, leaving her to hover alone in the sky, flapping her wings from time to time like one of those great leisurely birds that drift high up under the sun.

The steep slope to the Calvary was composed of meadows of poor grass and ledges of rock. The path wound around the rocks. The colours in spring and summer were grey and green, but on that day white and black. The ground was white and the little pine wood that circled the peak was black. Above the woods they saw the summit; it was bare but for the Cross, towards which the procession was moving. The little chimes joined Marie-Madeleine again, and now another sound could be heard. Timidly at first, then with more and more confidence, rose up the voices of the people climbing towards the cross. They asked; they appealed; they beseeched. "Aren't there three hundred of us? Surely our voices will be heard!" The priest, walking beneath a canopy, the white-robed men, the women reading from prayer books, other women leading children by the hand, old and crippled people who could scarcely walk, people with bandaged heads and some who were hiding their hands—everyone who could walk had joined the procession. No one was ashamed before God, not even those who had sores.

The procession slowly mounted the path that wound its way up the slope among snow-covered fields and rocks. Every now and then the progress of the cross was arrested because of the frozen snow, but it always moved on again resolutely, drawing the narrow stream of people after it. The energy to keep moving did not come from behind; the important thing was to look ahead, not backwards, and to climb higher and higher, one step after another. Then the sun rose and shone full upon them.

From there on the ascent was easy; in spite of themselves they seemed to be carried joyfully up the last bit of road and through the little pine wood. The cross was placed beneath the one already there, the canopy came to a halt and the people formed a circle.

They realised that they were alone in the presence of God. So high had they climbed that the loftiest peaks on the horizon seemed to be below them, and the neighbouring fields and villages were swallowed up in the depths. Their own village could scarcely be distinguished down behind them, its little grey roofs were so flat against the earth. In front opened out another valley so deep that nothing at all was visible, only a great misty emptiness. And the sky was everywhere, around and above them, and there was God in it, and the Son, and the Holy Ghost, and the Saints who had once been men and would understand them the better for that.

It was true that they had sinned, but were there any men on earth who had not? The thought of their sufferings filled them with self-pity; they fell on their knees and gazed up at the two crosses, the Virgin, and the banners. Then the praying began, the priest's voice mingling with their own. With some it took the form of silent supplication, but they all knelt on the stony ground with hands joined across their breasts and heads bent. They prayed a long time and felt that their words would be heard above.

"We had forgotten Thee, O Lord, but now our thoughts have come back to Thee. We know now why Thy hand has fallen so heavily upon us. It is because we deserve Thy punishment, and we thank Thee, O Lord, if this is Thy way of awakening in us a fitting respect for Thy Holy Name."

The bells were still ringing in the village below, and

happiness filled the hearts of all as they rose up and turned to descend the winding path. They did not believe they were the same people who had just climbed it. They looked without fear at the village, and on entering it they had the impression that it too had been kneeling. Their common enemy was there, but he would no longer harm them, and as they approached the open square many curious eyes looked in the direction of the Inn. First came the cemetery with its newly-made graves, so close to each other that they looked like successions of little white waves. Alas, this sight was only too well remembered. Too many places filled here, and too many empty ones at firesides, in beds, and at kitchen tables, too many pairs of strong arms so desperately needed! All this they saw, and regretted still, but it was not important now; one could rise above it.

They left the cemetery and turned the corner of the church. A song of joy burst from their lips as they advanced: first the cross, then the Virgin, the banners, and the canopy.

The square was deserted and the Inn closed, as they had expected. The curtains were drawn inside the windows and no smoke rose from the chimney. It had the look of a house long abandoned.

But the Man had only to open the door.

He simply lifted the latch, and the Host, whose golden ornaments shone behind its tiny crystal window, fell from hands that were no longer worthy to carry it. The next moment, the canopy, the cross, and the banners, and the silk-robed Virgin fell to the ground. The sky turned black, and the pigeons sailed down from the bell-tower on spread wings and flew away towards the valley.

CHAPTER VI

◊

Spring came too quickly that year and there were floods
and snow-slips. A general thaw brought this fresh
misfortune; there was destruction everywhere. The water
dug enormous gullies, walls fell in, and dams were overrun.
From the top of the bell-tower, the sight was terrifying.
Instead of the new green of spring and the little flower
gardens full of crocuses and anemones, great stretches of
gravel met the eye. The village looked as though a huge
plough had been dragged through it, and the sluices of the
pond had given away, so that its vase-shaped bottom now
looked like old crackle-ware. But the most astonishing
thing was the absence of living things—not even a cat
creeping under a barn door, or a hen tilting her red-
combed head. The bright April sun that usually fell upon
quickly budding bushes now only accentuated the frightful
desolation of it all. What emptiness! What a desert!

Not only were the streets empty but the fields as well,
and at this of all times in the year, when sowing has to be
done, and fences mended, and the fields harrowed or
rolled; a time when little girls make bouquets and when
lovers begin to go out together on Sunday evenings.
Everywhere on the hillsides something is going on. You
can imagine yourself alone but sooner or later a head
appears from behind a hedge; you go into the woods and
suddenly a man appears leading a cow harnessed to a farm-
cart. Now there was none of this sort of thing; a terrible
silence was everywhere. Down below in the valley and on
the other side of the mountain, life went on as usual, but
this afflicted village was wrapped in the silence of death.

Impassable roads, fields cut by deep gorges, and fallen trees marked the point beyond which it was not safe to venture. These boundaries had to be observed, for a curse had fallen on the village and the rumour had spread through the neighbourhood that it was the plague. Messengers were sent again to get help but the reply was: "One step nearer and we'll shoot!" So they were prisoners, all save the priest who had not been seen since the day of the procession.

The cawing of crows and other birds like them was the only sound to be heard now (all the little hedge birds had been devoured long ago) except for the unearthly bursts of laughter, snatches of song, and dance music that came from the Inn at night. There all was gaiety; more than a dozen men had now installed themselves where food and drink and women were plentiful. When a wine cask ran dry, the Man had only to touch it and it was full again. A big ham was taken down from the chimney and eaten to the bone. The Man stretched out his hand and immediately it had more meat on it than before. Money, though quite unnecessary because everything could be had for nothing, was to be acquired for the mere asking. The Man said, "Look at your purse." It was full of gold. Life was very pleasant, for this man who had been called Branchu and who now was The Master, could make whatever he liked out of nothing, as God could. He satisfied every need, he even created needs in order to satisfy them. The prettiest women in the village were there for the pleasure of the occupants of the Inn.

◊◊

Meanwhile a struggle with death went on in the village. A man, his wife and children, all in one bed! What was the use of getting up? It would only be a waste of the little strength they possessed, and that strength had to be carefully preserved. Pretty soon there would be no more to eat. What a pity the crops had been so good the year before, yielding such a plentiful supply of everything! Now the hay was spoiling, and the flour was mouldy in the bins. Almost all the beasts had died.

"Catherine!" It was Tronchet speaking, the richest land-owner in the parish, "Catherine, how much have we in the bank now?"

"Fifty-thousand francs!"

"Even that won't save us from starvation if this keeps up much longer." He looked at his wife lying beside him under the covers, and she turned her ashen grey face towards him, smiling a queer crazy smile. Fifty-thousand francs, and worth so many pebbles!

Old Jean-Pierre was sitting in his kitchen before a little fire of rubbish, when his wife called out to him:

"What's the matter?" he said.

"D'you think it's going to last much longer?"

"Can't tell. ..." A short silence followed.

"Jean-Pierre, why don't you say any more? I'm afraid, and you keep on sitting there, and not a word out of you."

"What's the use of being afraid? Faith's the thing." This was Jean-Pierre's favourite argument. His wife began to sob, for her faith was a feeble thing, and she wondered whether He, in whom she had put what faith she had, could possibly know of her existence.

Everywhere people were weeping. There was Clinche's wife and the five children whom he had abandoned. He had beaten her horribly, but when he had come in that night and said: "I'll be better off there than here with you," everything had been forgotten. Everything, if only he wouldn't go. He had laughed, saying, "Ah, that's it, you're

89

jealous. Well, this'll be a lesson to you. You can starve for all I care. They've got plenty of food where I'm going."

She had dropped to her knees clinging to him: "Oh, please, Clinche, for God's sake don't go there! Anywhere else, but not there!" It had not done any good, and now she was alone with her five children and nothing to eat. The youngest was just awake; he was only two, and she sat down on the bed where she had put them all. It was the only way she could keep them warm, for there was no more wood.

"What's the matter, my pet?" she asked, clasping him in her arms.

"Hungry," said the little voice. So she groped her way (there was no oil in her lamp) into the kitchen. In the cupboard there was only a half a bag of spoiled flour; she mixed some of it with water and took a cup of pap to the little fellow, but he refused to touch it and began to cry. The other children in the bed woke up and began to cry for bread.

"What am I going to do?" she asked despairingly. "Must I go and sell myself as he did?" Then she went on resolutely: "No, not that! I'd rather they'd die. I'll make them lie close to me and I'll hold their hands in mine and breathe on their faces. God! If only they could die peacefully, then I would be alone and I could die too with them dead all around me."

Farther down the street was Baptiste's house. He was the one whose thumb had become infected. The disease had gone up into his shoulder and now his body was a mass of putrefaction. There were green spots all over his stomach, but he laughed, saying to himself, "I thought I knew what disease would carry me off, but I was wrong. So much the worse for gangrene if hunger is winning the race. Gangrene would only have had to hurry a little."

In a hundred other houses it was the same. Many had to crawl on their hands and knees, being unable to stand. Their mouths were like the mouths of beasts; saliva ran down over their chins. Some bit into the floor-boards and tried to live on sawdust. Cats, dogs, and even mice had been killed; they had to be eaten raw for there was no firewood. Soon there were no animals left for them to kill, and the days of their existence could be counted. Eating raw flesh (it was almost like eating their own) doubled the violence of the disease: malignant ulcers in the case of grown-ups, and twisted arms and legs with children. There was not a house in the village that did not contain at least one corpse, for no one dared to go as far as the cemetery. A beloved father lies dead in a corner of the kitchen on the bare earthen floor; all that can be done is to put a cushion beneath his head. His family look the other way when passing so as not to see him. Little Julien, scarcely two years old, was put in a cardboard box. His father fetched a pot of paint and painted it blue. Perhaps he was trying to cheat Time in this way, unless indeed he was trying to cheat himself, for it did not take much thinking to realise how soon his own death would follow his son's. And there would probably be no coffin for him; to die unknown in some corner would be his fate.

Sounds of music and loud laughter still came from the Inn. Some of the village people peeped out, but only when it was quite dark, for they were ashamed. They slipped out through half-opened doors and made for the Inn.

A pleasant glow from its windows filled the square. All the windows were open and they hid in corners and behind walls, poking their heads out from time to time to gaze greedily into the bright interior. They saw tables covered with bottles and men sitting at the tables. Whenever the door opened, a warm puff of delicious smells came out, smells of meat and good things to eat. The outsiders could only bite into the food-laden air, but it was too much for them and a force they could not control dragged them by the shoulders and pushed them in at the Inn door. They burst into the wine room with arms raised, fell down on the floor, and rolled under the tables.

Someone shouted: "Here come some more of them!"

But they saw nothing, heard nothing, and it was only when food and drink were brought that they regained the power to understand what had happened. They devoured what was before them like starving dogs.

◊◊◊

That night there was a fete at the Inn. After the drinking came dancing, but the wine room was too small for it. One of the boys, called Labre, got out his mouth-organ and played a dance tune, but when the couples began to whirl about they bumped into the tables.

No one had any idea of the time, but the night must have been pretty well advanced. They were a bad lot, sleeping the day through and making day out of night; for them the moon took the place of the sun, and when there was no moon they always had the lamps to fall back upon. Their pleasure was of the sort that could best be enjoyed when curtained in by darkness. Thus the world was shut out; they were at cross purposes with it and felt that they had acquired a kind of topsy-turvy salvation. There were no prohibitions, and what they enjoyed most of all was freedom to do things hitherto impossible. And so when they had had more than their fill of food and drink (they only enjoyed over-eating and over-drinking now) they began to think of other distractions.

Someone suggested: "Let's go over to the church."

An excellent idea! Why hadn't that been thought of before? There would be plenty of room, and the idea of amusing themselves in a church, of all places, was one that appealed very strongly.

All they had to do was to cross the square; the door was open and they crowded in, pushing and elbowing each other, and pinching the women who screamed with delight.

"How are we going to see anything?" someone asked.

"By God, we'll light the candles."

One of the men climbed up on to the altar holding a lantern. The tabernacle and the monstrance fell to the floor, and that contributed to their pleasure. Matches were produced and the man on the altar struck one on his trousers. A tiny flame trembled at the top of one of the wax columns covered with golden traceries, and before long a whole row was burning brightly. Then they wanted to light the lamp of perpetual adoration, symbolic of the spirit that watched over them; it was hanging by a little chain from the high arched ceiling, but though there was plenty of oil in it their efforts were of no avail, and they ended by breaking it to bits upon the flagstones.

"That's the way to do it!" shouted Criblet who was leaning against one of the columns. "I stand aside from all this. Whoever it was who put me upon this earth (it must have been someone) said to one of my predecessors: 'You'll be a gardener,' to another, 'You'll be an Emperor,' to another, 'You'll be a beggar,' but when my turn came he didn't know what to tell me, so he said, 'You'll be Criblet, the others will do things and you'll just watch.' And he gave me a bottle to keep me from boring myself."

He produced this bottle from a pocket and there was a sound like water bubbling down the waste-hole in a drinking fountain. The chairs were thrown into one of the chapels and the dancing began. All went well except that Labre's mouth-organ was not loud enough. It was a small pocket one, meant only to be used in someone's kitchen when six or eight boys and girls wanted to dance on winter evenings, Sunday afternoons or holidays. It was loud enough for that, but in the lofty nave of the Church no one could hear it. Gentizon slipped out into the darkness.

Someone shouted, "Louder!" and Labre answered, "I'll bust my cheeks if I keep on like this! " Shoulders were shrugged and no further complaints were heard. In a few moments Gentizon appeared; he was not alone and they greeted him and his companion with cheers:

"Bravo! He's brought old Creux with him; just the thing!"

Gentizon was holding a little old man by the arm:

"I told him to bring his accordion along, that I was taking him to see some friends, and he must watch his step."

A burst of laughter followed this last remark, for old Creux was blind. He wagged his head comically, and when he smiled he bared his gums which were as pink as a little child's.

"Ye don't need to tell me to go to it; can't you see I'm glad to be here? Just keep on dancing."

They all crowded round him without his having the faintest idea how numerous the company was. He imagined himself in a barn or a dwelling house where he was usually taken and paid fifty centimes for his services. He grasped the accordion by the two ends with their brass keys. Between was the green leather bellows and old Creux pulled out two chords: "Are you ready?" He wore an old cap of rabbit skin and there was a smile upon his wrinkled face: "It's good to be at it again after so long."

A chair had been placed for him at the foot of one of

the columns and there was a bottle at his disposal. He turned and lowered his head till his ear almost touched the instrument, and his old fingers did their work so rapidly that it was almost impossible to see them. His foot beat time, his head swayed to and fro over his twinkling fingers, and the smile on his face came and went according to the difficulty of the passage he was playing. But the pleated leather bellows was never still—it stretched, contracted and twisted; and the couples whirled round and round.

There were almost as many women as men, and they clasped each other tightly; faces got redder and redder and the sound of quickly drawn breath could be heard. No one understood the reason for such furious dancing. None of the quiet old-fashioned steps were even thought of—those dances where, after a figure was over, a kiss was sought in a dark corner and generally refused. They held each other so closely that they had the appearance of having grown together, and some of the couples looked as though they were writhing in agony.

Old Creux kept smiling and his music flowed on steadily, except during the few seconds it took him to swallow some drink and start a fresh tune. There were polkas and mazurkas, and fast waltzes that made the interlacing legs of the dancers look like branches blowing in the wind. Candles were knocked over from time to time, and when a draught blew in through the broken windows, the flames on the ones left standing bent over sideways, causing tears of hot wax to run down upon the altar. The people shouted and laughed: "Let's take the lid off!"

"Come on, Felicie, I'm tired waiting."

"All right, Louis, I'm ready. Buzz me around hard."

Shirts, collars, and vests were torn off; everyone was hot; some came to a sudden stop and threw out their arms laughing hysterically, and now it was hard to tell whether they laughed or sobbed. It was unmixed happiness, and they felt like little birds that had just broken out of their shells. They had known slavery, but all that was past now. They indulged their absolute freedom:

"What is there to stop me from taking you in my arms before everybody, Felicie? Just think what trouble it used to be even to speak to you. I was always afraid someone would see us together. What stops me from picking up this chair and throwing it at the window?"

They felt the need to destroy things, and before long the need was satisfied; so much so that it was as if they had wished to bring about their own destruction. Many sank to the floor completely exhausted. A few managed to get on to chairs where they sat with their mouths hanging open and their hands pressed against their chests. In a few moments, however, things began to move again, and there was soon another whirling of hugging and kissing couples. Sweat poured down from their faces and a shout for more drink resulted in a fresh cask of wine. It was rolled across the nave and placed upon an overturned confessional. Then a tap was inserted and dry throats were refreshed. After touching glasses they formed a circle around the cask, and old Creux, though tired of his accordion, was prepared to keep going. "Are you through?" he asked suddenly. "Come along; I'll play another one—the best of all." So they began again with new vigour, and one of the women detached herself from the crowd and stood near the altar with her hands on her hips. It was Lucie, a big red-cheeked girl, and she laughed a coarse laugh, standing there in the dim light of the few remaining candles:

"I'm tired of the whole lot of you. I'd like a change. I've danced with 'em all and they've all kissed me. Do I have to start over again?" She was only a little too fond of pleasure;

she simply followed her physical desires blindly, and this was why she had been among the first to go to the Inn. Now she was beginning to be bored; she had experienced all these things before and she yawned:

"It's nothing but the same thing over and over again! What shall I do?" She pushed all the men away: "No, not you, or you, or you." She stretched out her arms slowly, then drew them in and covered her face with her hands.

"I'll tell you, Lucie," someone said, "if you don't think we're good enough for you..."

He pointed: "That'll be just the thing! A woman hard to please should be given a new partner who hasn't been dancing."

"Do you want him?" they asked.

She held out her arms and there was a rush towards the wall where a tall Crucifix was hanging. The figure was yellow with red marks on the hands and feet. The head rested on one shoulder and the stomach fell inwards beneath the ribs. The nails were soon drawn out of the hands and feet, and the Christ was lifted down, and placed upright upon the floor. Lucie walked towards it and they asked her:

"Will he do?"

She threw back her head and her eyes flashed, but then she hid her face with her arm as though ashamed. It was a gesture of great desire mingled with timidity. They called to Creux: "Is it your best that you're playing now?" Creux did not answer, but a cascade of little clear notes poured away from his nimble fingers and the dancing recommenced, with Lucie and her partner leading off.

The day dawned, but no one noticed it until a strong light filled the church. The music stopped and every one turned instinctively to look at Lucie; she was laying stretched out upon the floor where she had fallen beneath the weight of the Christ. She seemed powerless to regain her feet, either because of the weight of the figure or because her legs would no longer support her. Every time she tried to get up she fell back again, and her hysterical laughing rang through the church.

Though every one's legs were very unsteady, Lucie was lifted up and given support, for the moment of departure had arrived. It was the light of day that drove them from the church. There was nothing breakable that had not been broken; the pictures of the Saints and those showing the Way of the Cross had been torn from the walls and kicked into shreds. Here and there the debris was knee high. The walls alone were undamaged, except for a crevice in the eastern one.

Traces of the festivities were everywhere; the last wine-cask was staved in and its contents had covered the floor with slippery pools.

Lucie and the Christ were placed upon a stretcher formed of shoulders and uplifted hands. A feeling of bravado took possession of them all as they approached the church door; they would show the powers above what kind of people they were, that they had done what it had pleased them to do. Two or three village people met them as they emerged into the square, and asked for food and drink, but they were told to go to the Inn; and the procession moved onwards, defying the daylight with its double burden.

The sky was cloudless and hardly a breath of wind was stirring; for them it seemed to be a sign that nothing was forbidden, or ever would be, after that. The calm blue was above them, and the stillness of death was upon the earth. Silence everywhere; not a sound; nothing…except the Man at the door of the Inn. He asked them: "Everything all right?" Then, "I can see it is. Well, all you have to do is to begin over again." And he laughed while speaking these last words.

◊◊◊◊

So they began again. But in the village, people who were able prayed before their crucifixes all day long. In spite of their recent failure to obtain assistance from above, they persisted in praying, for it was the only thing left for them to do—the only thing they could do. And they said to themselves that it would perhaps be wiser to do singly what they had done together. A prayer might be more easily heard if it were spoken by one person. So they got out their rosaries and told them with long emaciated fingers.

Old Jean-Pierre was the most diligent of them all. He knelt by his bed from morning until evening and often all through the night. His clasped hands were stretched towards the statue on the wall and the spray of box in its pewter vessel, and every prayer that he knew issued from his lips. When he came to the end, he began all over again, and when his wife asked him for water he did not hear her. She was unable to move and death hovered about her. One could almost hear its rattle as she called out, and her finger nails scratched the bed clothes. Jean-Pierre heard nothing but his own vain words; his wife died a few days later, and he was barely conscious of the fact. His obstinate praying kept everything else out of his mind. And in all the other little rooms, dark and evil-smelling, it was the same thing. Joseph, alone, said, "What can it matter now?" They wondered how he had escaped death, and they soon began to wonder how it was that any of them had escaped. Every day it got worse, and a pedlar, coming down from the hills with the intention of making a round of the village, said to a friend:

"What a good thing I stopped in time! The place has turned into a cemetery full of crows and other birds who live on spoiled meat. The infection will spread if we're not careful." But no one went there, and in the neighbourhood people wondered if all the inhabitants were dead.

They were not all dead, but something worse was happening. Every day more people gave in. At first they had presented themselves at the Inn singly, now they went in groups. The temptation was too great; their physical and moral resistance had vanished. In the beginning they had said, "We must be true to the great Law-giver even at the expense of our lives." Now it was: "Perhaps life is the most precious thing we have."

A choice had to be made. How could they think about their souls now? Their bodies' need was too urgent. The failure of the procession had almost convinced them that they were abandoned by God, and they wondered whether it was worth while praying to him anymore. And if they had been abandoned by God, would it not be better to put themselves under the protection of another? If they did not, what was left but loneliness and a hideous death? Every mind was filled with thoughts like these. The miser wondered what good his money was to him; lazy persons said to themselves that there would be no more work to avoid; those who were dependent upon bodily pleasures and had long been deprived of them felt the need more bitterly every day. The greedy had visions of delicious food, the drunkard of drink, and the temptations of the flesh increased in violence until men groaned with the desire for satisfaction. They were like cows lowing for grass in winter. Anger flamed up in the hearts of some; there were blasphemous accusations of the Heavenly Throne, and dissension arose among them. Other diseases began to appear—black lumps at people's necks that ended by killing them. Always more deaths, more bodies unburied, and less and less flour in the bins.

In the streets the Inn people could be heard singing. They knocked at doors and shouted:

"Hey, in there, can't you make up your minds? Is it pleasant to die like that, when you can come along with us and be happier than you ever were in the old days? The price isn't high—only the sign of the cross backwards. You enter and the Master says: 'Do that.' And you do it. Then you get as fat and rosy as we are."

They did have a well-fed look, and the slightest crack in the curtains enabled those behind them to see men and women wearing good clothes—a round-faced, full-lipped, bright-eyed gathering. They knocked a second time, and the door usually remained shut, but sometimes it was opened.

"Bravo, another one!" they would shout as the shrinking recruit joined the ranks. And this was what happened to Amelie. She heard the voices of some men she used to dance with. They had come to get her.

"You remember us, don't you, Amelie? Aren't you going to dance with us anymore? It's different now from what it was before. We can do what we want. Come along, be a good girl."

She had been lying on the floor, and she raised her head and listened. Her parents were in the same room, but her father was out of his mind and barely able to breathe. Her mother was motionless and silent. Amelie sat up now; she remembered the man who was calling to her, for she had often danced with him, and on many a Sunday evening they had walked home in the moonlight together from a party. These memories filled her mind with indecision. "What if I go with them?" she thought. "It hasn't hurt him at all."

She argued therefore that it would be all right for her,

and to be in his company would be so nice. For a moment more she hesitated like a ripe apple about to drop from the tree, then she made up her mind and got upon her knees. She could see that her father had not moved, and her mother looked as though she were asleep. Outside the voice kept on calling; she stood up with an effort, turned toward the door, and, passing the mirror, she was terrified at the deep black circles around her eyes. "Ah, well," she thought, "he'll understand." In a moment she had arranged her hair, but nothing more, for the voice was still calling. She found the door locked with a double turn, and, while trying to manipulate the big key that had rusted in the lock, she suddenly heard another sound, a wail out of the heavy silence of death; at that moment the voice in the street became silent.

"Don't go! Don't go!" And again, "Don't go! Don't go!"

Then there was silence but for the sound of bare footsteps upon the floor behind her. She could not open the door and the possessor of the beseeching voice behind her laid her hands on her daughter's shoulders. She stood there for a moment in her chemise, an old, thin, wizened woman; then she spoke:

"Amelie, please, you know what's waiting for you there. Think of the tortures and the punishment you will have to suffer afterwards—the fire and brimstone. They last forever!"

Amelie freed herself violently from the old woman's embrace, breaking the bonds of flesh and blood, and the key turned in the lock. Her mother lay on the floor now, so she slid back the bolt. She felt hands clutching at her feet and, turning abruptly, she clenched her fist and struck the upturned face beneath tangled strands of grey hair ...she could hear the voice in the street:

"Someone's opened the door; it's her—hurry up, my little pet. You'll see how we'll look after you."

The crowd moved off in the direction of the Inn and another gang came out of another street. A son called to his mother, a husband to his wife, sisters to sisters, brothers to brothers, and finally a whole family came out to join them: Father, mother, and five children. They approached with bowed heads, holding one another by the hand. The father spoke to one of the second gang in low tones:

"We stuck it out as long as we could, but look at them; they're too little to die yet. Do what you like with us."

They were taken like the others to the Inn and the father was told to cross himself backwards. This he did, and his wife, and the children too, but they did not understand what they had done. Food was brought, and what joy it was for them! Soup, macaroni, meat, and then every description of cake which they hardly dared to touch. There were chocolate cakes, vanilla cream-cakes, and some with little stars of candied fruit on them. They hesitated, but were told to eat whichever they liked. Little hands stretched out and bright eyes shone with pleasure.

How nice it was to get away from stuffy rooms full of foul air into this gay crowd seated around the big table. There was nothing to worry about, full bottles were plentiful, and someone was playing a mouth-organ.

Criblet was installed in a corner with Clinche, but they did not seem to be hitting it off very well.

"Keep still," grumbled Clinche; "you talk too much." He had been drinking a lot and this always made him melancholy. Criblet, on the contrary, became more and more cheerful:

"I'm free, anyway," he cried. "You're tied up with a wife and children."

"I was," replied Clinche, "but now I'm like you." Criblet shrugged his shoulders. This was the way all their squabbles began; Clinche pretended he was like Criblet and Criblet always put him in his place.

Clinche struck the table with his fist:

"After all's said and done, what are you? What did you ever do? Suppose you had to support someone. You haven't any money nor any way to earn money, so cut out the big talk." He tried to laugh, but Criblet replied coolly, as was his custom:

"You don't know really anything about me."

Clinche got up and it looked as though he were about to let fly at Criblet, but the Man knew how to keep order. He had only to raise his hand.

They were there to enjoy one another's company peaceably. The sun was shining outside and it fell upon the plates on the table, and the wine in the glasses gleamed a brighter yellow. Every one talked gaily, telling stories and experiences. They boasted of things they used to be ashamed of, and concealed what they had always spoken of with pride.

"I've robbed my father."

"I've deceived my mother."

A farmer put water in his milk, or gave bad weight of hay. A miller mixed his flour with plaster. They invented crimes they had not committed in order not to look ridiculous, but they especially enjoyed boasting.

Trente-et-Quarante was there too and this was his contribution:

"He was ten months old and one day he smiled at me. One of his cheeks was red and the other was white because he had just been sucking. His face looked like an apple; red and white and smiling. I put him in a strong linen bag and he screamed and kicked when I started off. I had his head under my arm and I held his feet with my hand. I felt something breaking, but I had to hurry. It had all been thought out; I went to the middle of the bridge where the water looked pretty in the moonlight. Clouc! That's what it sounded like and the stone took it down quickly; I only saw it for a minute in the water. The bag with the kid inside it sank, and my thirty francs rose up—it cost me that much a month to keep him. Now, wasn't I right to do it? Wasn't it a good job?"

He emptied his glass in one gulp and every one followed his example; they were really getting drunk. Things began to have strange colours: blue, green, orange, and red. Little bits of sunlight like pieces of ripe fruit whirled in and out of their vision. The table collapsed, and the glasses and bottles rolled on to the floor, but the laughter was so loud that no one heard anything, and in the confusion the fallen table was hardly noticed.

In front of the Inn, men were stretched upon the ground sound asleep. Too much food and drink and other pleasures! Some lay on their sides; some on their stomachs; and others on their backs with their eyes shaded from the sun. Big Lucie was completely exhausted and her clothes were barely hanging on her. The church, a few steps away, was a frightening thing to look at. The great door was torn from its hinges; the walls were cracked; and the bell-tower was leaning. But the village was a far more terrifying sight, with its caved-in roofs, upturned streets and corpses thrown out like garbage.

Another troupe came down by one of the steep mountain roads: "We've got three more." They were being carried because they could not walk: two men and a woman. At the Inn they were received by the Man, and they crossed themselves backwards as the others had done:

"Do you know who I am?" he laughed. "There is no longer any good or evil. You must obey the powers of earth now, and renounce the powers above." All of them there had done this, and the Man laughed again and repeated:

"There is no longer any good or evil."

Everyone but Lhôte laughed with him because slaves follow their master. Lhôte had been silent for days. He seemed to be out of everything, and his face was pale; his eyes had grown larger and his beard blacker and longer.

The Man called to him:

"And you, Lhôte, what do you think?"

Lhôte looked up. "Who do you think I am, Lhôte?"

"I think you are Christ," he answered gravely, "and you manifest yourself in ways that seem right to you."

"My poor Lhôte, you've made a mistake. Watch now."

He went to the window and raised his hand; a black cloud rapidly stretched itself across the sky and a clap of thunder was heard, "You see!"

Lhôte shook his head: "I tell you that you are Christ all the same, because the dead obeyed you."

CHAPTER VII

◊

They said little Marie Lude was able to do what she did now because she alone was free from fear. She went away with her mother, if you remember, at the beginning of the winter. The people treated them badly, and one day when it was snowing they left the village. The mule carried their belongings, and those big red-headed birds flew out of the hedges. They went to their little house far up above the village, and they knew nothing of what had happened. There they had been, the two of them quite alone, away from everything. The winter came and went, and they stayed on in ignorance of all the misfortunes below in the village. Lude, the third member of the family, the father, was forced to leave the village before they did, because he had moved his boundary stones. The spring found him still wandering about near the place where he had known happiness and where there would never be happiness for him again. His crime enforced a restless existence upon him; it deprived him of his home and at the same time he found he had not the courage to go away altogether. He was continually on the move, skirting the village, approaching and stopping, always at a certain distance from it, for he thought, "How could I ever be forgiven?"

No one ever knew how he had kept alive during that time, for he was always hesitating between two things: to go away altogether, which he could not bring himself to do, or to come back, which was impossible.

Weeks and months passed, and one day he was sitting beneath a big red-trunked fir tree. His beard had grown down to his waist, and his hair hung down just as far in back. He sat and waited. But what did he expect would happen after all these months? It was time to get up and move on, but he did not get up, and his head bent farther and farther forward. Suddenly he threw it back, and, being unable to endure the silence any longer, he called out, and his voice echoed again and again through the forest.

◊◊

That same morning Marie was sitting on a green slope while the goat cropped grass near her. It was just another day in the long chain of time. The winter had come and gone and the soft round note of the cuckoo could be heard in the woods nearby. The grass was growing fast and there were flowers scattered through it. It was a long day—the longest of the year.

Suddenly while Marie sat watching her goat, she thought she heard someone calling her. She looked up, but saw only the goat pulling out tufts of grass and shaking its white beard. At the top of the green slope came the sky like a blue painted veiling. She wondered if she had been mistaken, but no, there it was again—

"Marie!"

And again:

"Marie! Marie!"

The great moment for her had arrived, and she did not hesitate. She had heard the call, and now she must go. But still she could see no one; she looked everywhere but ...nobody. "It must be *him*," she said to herself resolutely. In a moment she had thought it out: the goat could be left quite well and her mother would worry about her, but that didn't matter, for wouldn't she bring *him* back with her?

Off she went down the long mountain path. It was a

difficult path to follow, but she knew it by heart, through all its turnings, its risings, and its descents. A wood had to be crossed, then a wide meadow, then another wood. Often there was no path at all beneath the trees, but she could always see where it began again. From time to time she stopped for an instant, and the voice urged her forward.

Traces of the tragedy she was approaching began to appear, and they would have frightened her had she noticed them. Some white oaks that had fallen across the road caused her no astonishment and she did not even slacken her pace. All she had to do was to creep under them. Then the light changed and the very air became empty and soundless; no more birds singing; no church bells tolling in the village or cow-bells tinkling in the fields.

She kept on without noticing anything until the last ridge above the village was climbed; then the full horror of it came to her, A smell of putrefaction rose to her nostrils as from open graves, and there was not only the smell but the appearance of open graves: debris of walls torn from their foundations and huge piles of upturned earth. Grey deathlike silence was everywhere; she was conscious of it, but did not hesitate.

The first sign of life was when she passed the miller's house; its walls were cracked and the moss-covered mill wheel had ceased to turn. A voice questioned her:

"Where are you going?"

Marie looked up and saw that it was the miller's wife leaning from a window; the woman was so changed that she hardly recognised her.

"Don't go any farther or it'll be the end of you!"

"Have you seen him?"

The miller's wife shook her head and Marie went on into the village. Windows were thrown open and people cried out:

"Stop, don't go any farther! You don't know what it's like."

Marie paid no heed to these warnings for she had just caught sight of a head peering out from behind a wall. She thought he was watching her, but that he had not the courage to show himself. The head was withdrawn and she said, "I'll go as far as our house anyhow." It was therefore necessary for her to cross the square and this she did in spite of further warnings. A few people were courageous enough to come out into the street; was it because they wanted to stop her, or had they perceived the light that seemed to cling about her and felt the puffs of fresh air that had begun to blow down from the hills?

In the square, meanwhile, those who had been lying asleep began to wake up. One after another raised a sleepy head, yawned, and let it fall again. They had slept out upon the ground because it was suffocating indoors. Beneath the big lime-tree they were lying higgledy-piggledy, just where sleep had overtaken them the night before. And now pleasure had come again to find them.

Another day had dawned like all the others, and the great stark tree which looked as though it had been carved with a chisel out of black stone, still stretched its motionless branches over them. Some were laying upon bundles of straw like animals, others upon the bare ground. There were more than a hundred and fifty of them; men, women and children—Criblet, Clinche, Big Lucie, the man with his wife and five children, Trente-et-Quarante, Labre, Gentizon, and Lhôte too, though he kept himself away from the others.

Candles still burned in the wine-room, and upon the tables little shining pools of wine dripped through the cracks on to the floor, making a sound like clocks ticking in the emptiness. And every now and then one of the candles crackled, spluttered, and went out.

Outside, where people lay about like the killed on a battlefield, arms began to stretch, knees were pulled up, and bodies turned over with sighs and yawns. Even in sleep they began to make ready for a day of pleasure as others might prepare for work.

"Where's your accordion. Father Creux? A little music, please. We make it our business to enjoy life, and we like to see your old face bending over till it almost touches the bellows and your fingers dancing over the keys. Only you'll have to wait for us to wake up."

They were still half asleep when Marie drew near, and at first no one saw her; it would have been quite easy had they been capable of seeing anything, and they must have heard windows opening and warnings being shouted at her: "Don't go any farther! Stop! Stop!" The village began to rouse itself, and the silence that had rested upon it for so long was broken.

Marie drew near, and it was Gentizon who saw her first. He propped up his head on his elbow and poked Labre who lay next to him. At first they did not recognise her and Gentizon simply remarked:

"Here comes another," But when she was close to them he cried: "It's impossible! Marie! Lude's daughter! But it is Marie. Ages since we saw her, and Lude, he's not been seen again."

Then he added: "How pretty she is now!"

The thing started like that. Labre and Gentizon looked at each other and silently agreed to act together. The truth was that neither of them could get to his feet alone, so they lifted each other up and laughed as they stood there before her; but what they hoped would come next made them laugh louder still.

Marie watched them walk a few steps and was astonished at their height. Swaying back and forth, like trees detached from their roots, they stretched out their arms to her and she noticed their decayed teeth and puffy red eyes.

"Come on, Marie," they said, "you've been away for such a long time!"

She hesitated, unable to make out what the peculiar expression on their faces meant. The others sat up, rubbed their eyes and looked at her. They looked queer too, and laughed the same laugh. She was frightened and hurried on.

Labre and Gentizon shouted, "Bravo!" and, being the only ones standing, they had the lead on the others. They followed Marie with long awkward steps, but were unable somehow to get anywhere near her. The others followed her too, and Labre and Gentizon understood that they had no time to lose. Gentizon made a lunge but missed his mark and rolled into the gutter. Labre followed her closely and every one said, "He'll get her." He seemed steadier and to have better calculated his movements, but at the moment of overtaking her he fell backwards as though he had encountered a stone wall.

The others stood still; silence fell upon the square, and the sound of voices in the village could be heard again. Did they fear Marie, or was it pity?

Perhaps it was just curiosity, but whatever the cause, it was evident that the village had stirred from its deathlike silence. The good news spread mysteriously through the streets. Could it be true? Was it possible? People came out fearlessly into the open, and there was no more furtive peeping through cracks and half-drawn curtains.

In the square they began to be impatient, especially the women: "Go and find the Master," they cried; "she's making fun of us, but she'll soon see…"

They were surprised that he did not appear, and while someone went into the Inn to get him, Criblet leaned from one of the windows: "I'm just watching. I'm out of all this."

A knock at the door brought the Man to the threshold.

"You'll see! You'll see!" the women shouted to Marie. Then the Man came forward a few steps, hesitated, then a few steps more. He seemed to have lost some of his assurance and he wore a forced smile. He moved very slowly and a little unsteadily, to the astonishment of those who watched him. Then his skin began to wrinkle, seeming to detach itself from his face and neck and arms; it hung about him, loosely, like a garment that would soon fall from his body.

Now he stood quite still; Marie walked up to him and all she had to do was to cross herself—to make the true sign. A crash of thunder tore through the silence…

A real glow spread over the sky, it was afterwards related, and the earth shook so violently that the houses were in danger of complete destruction. Then, silence again, and looking from their windows the people could scarcely believe their eyes. But there it was, and the sunlight poured down brightly upon it: a new village, with walls and roofs mended, and fresh paint everywhere. The brightest sun that had been seen for months and a prettier village than ever—a village in its Sunday clothes!

For a long time their amazement kept them from thinking, but at last they understood:

"It's Marie!"

Everyone wanted to see her, and the living rose up from

amongst the dead. The streets began to fill with people. Some of them could not walk and were carried, others used crutches, and there were still others who crawled along on their knees. It did not matter how they went; to get there was the thing. Already the diseases they were suffering from had begun to disappear, and their bodies, like the houses, became strong and healthy again. Those who had been bent over stood upright once more; eruptions, black ulcers and open sores vanished, and fresh clear-eyed faces drank in the glistening sunlight.

They were astonished to find no one in the square—not even the bodies of those whom they expected to see. It was quite empty and no signs of disorder were visible; no doubt the earth had opened and swallowed them up. Another surprise, and a far greater one, awaited them: she whom they had come to find was nowhere to be seen.

Vainly they searched for her and asked each other where she could be; no one knew. And a great uneasiness took possession of them; it was as though they had been abandoned a second time

At that moment someone cried out: "There she is!" and all was forgotten. There was a rush towards the narrow street where she had appeared. She was coming from her house and the people surged around her, longing to speak, but not daring to utter a word. Still, it did not matter; they could at least look at her and touch her.

But now another surprise. She herself seemed anxious about something, and she asked hopelessly, "Haven't you seen him, either? Haven't any of you met him anywhere? I've been to our house, but...he wasn't there."

The people fell on their knees, and the women nearest her kissed the edge of her skirt.

He had, alas, never dared to show himself, and even now when the village had come to life again and every one had been forgiven, he still hesitated, saying to himself, "Perhaps they deserve to be forgiven, but I don't."

So they went to find him, and, when he was brought to where Marie stood, he threw himself face downwards upon the ground before her.

"Is it you, father? Is it really you?"

He could not answer, and covering his face with his hands he wept bitterly. Marie knelt down and leaned over him, taking his hands in hers.

At that moment Big Marie-Madeleine was heard; there was no one in the bell-tower, but the air vibrated with the deep-toned music of her voice, and the little bells sent forth cascades of silvery notes. After weeks of silence they were ringing now of their own accord: first Marie-Madeleine, then the little ones, mounting higher and higher towards the sun.

Marie helped him to his feet. "She's waiting for us, Father," she said, and he told her he was ready, that he had the courage to go now. So Marie and her father set forth. The sound of the chimes preceded them and the people followed, but it was not a procession like the other one, because peace had come to them and gladness filled their hearts in spite of the sorrow and affliction they had passed through. It was a smaller procession this time, but their troubles were all forgotten; indeed it was as though they had risen from death. The President came first, then Communier, old Jean- Pierre, and the rest. The way led past meadows dotted with flowers and they threw back their heads and stretched wide their arms for joy. Even Joseph Amphion was comforted, for while gazing into the sky, he thought he saw the beloved one he had lost. They were just entering the forest, and raising his eyes, he had seen her figure floating in the blue just above the tree tops.

◊◊◊◊

They were so oblivious to everything but their happiness that they had not noticed poor Lhôte when, passing the Church. He had been spared because he alone had been innocent of evil. He was lying in a comer of the churchyard with his face hidden in his hands.

One day, the following autumn, while hunting, Bonvin found the priest at the bottom of a ravine. He was hanging from the branch of a larch tree, and he had neither eyes, nose, nor mouth. His whole face had gone, for crows had come and had known what to do.

Ω

www.ingramcontent.com/pod-product-compliance
Lightning Source LLC
Chambersburg PA
CBHW050901180626
46814CB00007B/2835